HIGH SCHOOL BOYS
AND THE SILVER LEGION

Joshua Mancini

PAGE PUBLISHING
Conneaut Lake, PA

First originally published by Page Publishing 2024

ISBN 979-8-89315-469-6 (pbk)
ISBN 979-8-89315-477-1 (digital)

Printed in the United States of America

For Zachary Hayden Tupin

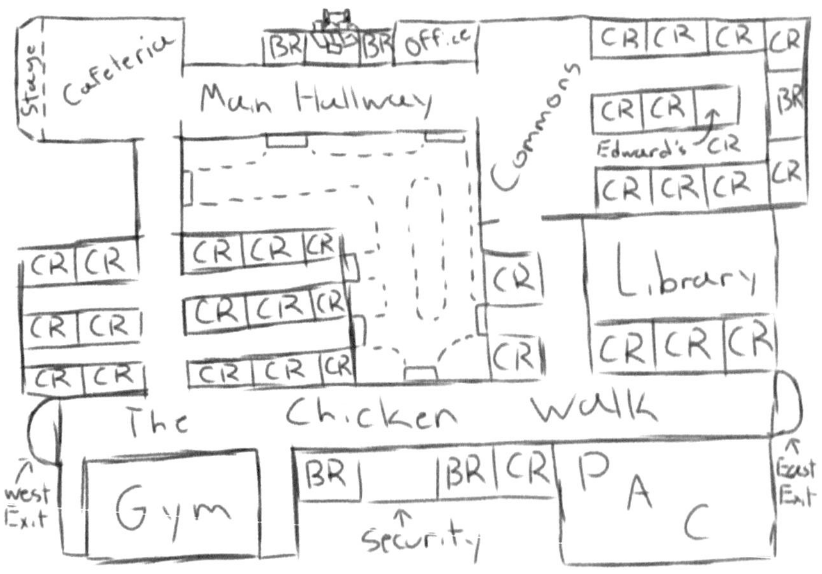

Shady Springs High School campus map
BR, bathroom
CR, classroom

Thud…thud…thud. Her shins started to bleed as she got dragged down seemingly endless stairs. *Thud…thud…thud.* Each shin got slammed into the metal. *Thud…Thud…Thud.* Two men were beside her, each holding one of her arms, yanking her down each and every step. The girl was forced to be there. The men? They were paid to be there.

The stairs were metal with a red border, cold and wet. They went down in a triangular pattern fully surrounded by a bleak-gray concrete wall. It was dark except for the dim-yellow LED on every other step. The men wore a black tunic with black pants. They each had a rifle tied to a black strap that was loosely wrapped around their body, swaying back and forth as they descended each step.

When they got to the bottom of the stairs, the men threw the girl against the wall. One of the men quickly pulled out his rifle and shouted, "Don't move!" The other man calmly walked over to the wall on their right. The girl's body tightened up in fear as she could see inside the barrel of the gun pointed right at her. The other man, not pointing the rifle, gently placed his hand on the concrete wall. Its cold and rough touch didn't surprise him, as if he had done this before. A moment later, a panel extended out of the wall. The panel was gray, like everything else, and had buttons, similar to what you would see on a cash register. The man with the rifle kept his stance as the other man proceeded to push a series of buttons on the panel that extended off the concrete wall. A ding sound went off, and then the wall where the girl was forced up against started to open very slowly like sliding doors, filling the room with the sound of grinding, clanking metal. But that sound was drowned out by what was behind this wall: a big blue circular portal with unreadable writing all along the edges, although the girl could make out the number *3* on the top of the portal's edge. Screams came out of it, and a deep hum echoed through the room.

"Go in," the man pointing the gun said harshly. He pointed the gun to the portal and then back at her.

"Wait, Mr. Wi—" she started to say but got cut off by a warning shot that just nicked her ear and flew into the portal behind her.

"Once you're in, you are to look for a portal very similar to this one," the man next to the panel said. "Once you find it and are able to get to and from it," he emphasized, "then you can come back here and go home." He finished, calmly.

"But—"

"No buts. Go…now." The man with the rifle's voice grew long and deep.

She stood up straight and looked at the portal, back at the men, and then the portal again. She reached through the blue portal and let her hand get absorbed by the cold gooey gel that made up this gateway. It felt as if she was sticking her hand into ice-cold Jello. She quickly pulled her hand out and was about to wipe the goo off on her shirt, but to her surprise, her hand was completely clean, and nothing was on it. The man holding the rifle started to fidget with the trigger and even began to line up a shot. The girl noticed this in the corner of her eye, so with a few deep breaths and her back turned to the men, she walked through, and the men watched as the portal engulfed her.

The man lowered his rifle. The other man at the panel pushed more buttons, and suddenly, the wall in front of the portal started to close, making those same old metallic noises. The screams and deep hum slowly vanished as the wall closed itself. The men looked at each other, exchanged looks of congratulations, and slowly walked back over to the stairs. In front of the stairs was a red and silver caged locker with more rifles inside it. The men put their guns in the locker, locked it up, and started making the long journey upstairs. Once they got to the top, they opened the door to see four school buses dropping kids off. They locked the door behind them.

"We got to get quicker at that," one of the men said.

"Relax, just a few more weeks before the purge," the other man added.

"We need to push it up, Dr. B. Perry and the security guard are having a meeting today," he stated.

"Then deal with it!" Dr. B said. "She was the last one until the purge anyway, all right?"

The other man let out a deep sigh.

"I'll see you at band practice, yeah?"

"Yeah," the man said, his eyes pointing down, "see ya."

The men split off into different directions and went on their way. Dr. B walked away from the buses and toward his office at the other end of the building, while the other man walked toward the buses on his way to the main office.

"Hey, Mr. Willy!" one of the kids getting off the bus shouted to the man supposably named Mr. Willy, as he was walking toward the front of the school.

"Hey, Lucas, how's it going!" Mr. Willy responded.

"I'm good. How are you?" the kid named Lucas asked as he ran right next to Mr. Willy and continued walking with him.

"I'm doing pretty good, Lucas. Thanks for asking. Say, are you ready for that trumpet test today?"

"I was born ready for this test, Mr. Willy!"

They both chuckled as they walked by a big concrete sign planted in the grass that read *Shady Springs High School*. More buses came, more students parked their cars, and more kids flooded into their high school, all of them unaware of what lay right beneath their feet.

CHAPTER 1

High School Boys and the Silver Legion

It was 7:00 a.m., and Luke was in his room, looking down out the window, watching his bus drive right past his street. This didn't surprise him though; his dad usually drove him to school. Luke had his black backpack on with black basketball shorts and a gray T-shirt.

"Dad?" he called out. There was no answer. Luke rolled his eyes, left his room, and went through the hallway into the master bedroom. His dad was lying asleep alone on his king-sized bed. The alarm clock on his nightstand was blaring. Luke walked up to the alarm clock and turned it off. On his father's nightstand, next to the alarm clock, was his dad's journal. It was black, and Luke noticed the pencil stuffed in the middle of the pages. As far as Luke knew, his father wrote in that journal every night. Luke didn't know why; he didn't know what his father wrote about or who he was writing it for. All he knew was that he wasn't allowed to read it. It was the only part of his father's life he knew nothing about, but Luke rarely ever thought about his father's journal apart from the times he noticed the journal in his father's room. With the alarm clock off, Luke slowly leaned over his dad.

"Dad!" His dad's eyes opened up, just a little, to see a kid standing over his face. The first thing Luke's dad noticed was his son's dark hair not being combed, but at this point, it was so long he knew Luke wouldn't even bother trying to comb it.

"Dad!" Luke started to shake the bed. "Dad, wake up. I'm going to be late for school."

"Should have taken the bus," his dad replied, closing his eyes again.

"Then who would tell you to get off your ass and go to work?"

"Luke, language!"

"Dad, school," Luke said, still shaking the bed. "If you don't get up, how are we going to get to school, and how are you going to get paid?"

"Money?" his dad's eyes finally opened again.

"You know that's what jobs are for right?"

Luke's Dad got up, got dressed, and got ready for school as well, carrying a briefcase with his journal and his laptop in it. No one knew that he brought his journal with him to work every day, but he knew he would never let that journal out of his sight.

Luke waited in the living room, scrolling through videos on his phone, as his father jaunted down the stairs.

"Come on, let's go!" His father sounded exhausted as he said it.

"About time!" Luke said.

They both hopped into his dad's truck and headed off for school. The truck was blue and only had a driver and passenger's seat, though you could fit a third person in the middle if you squeezed. At a red light on their way to school, Luke's Dad asked, "What day is it?"

"Thursday," Luke said in a mundane tone.

"Thursday!" He yelled. He stomped on the acceleration peddle even though the light was still red. "Dr. B is going to kill me!" Luke's dad yelled as he swerved around car after car.

Luke looked at the cars behind them. "With this driving, YOU'RE going to kill ME!"

Luke's dad ran through the final stop sign, without looking either way, and smoothly drove straight into the students' parking lot, at least as smooth as you can going fifty miles per hour. Luke's dad was allowed to park in the teachers' parking lot, but Luke's friends always parked in the top right of the students' parking lot, and they always hung out around there before and after school. So Luke's dad parked up there so his son could hang out with his friends.

His dad put the car in park and yanked the keys out of the ignition. "Bye!" he said abruptly as he opened his door, slammed it shut, and sprinted toward the back of the building. He never did that. Even on Thursdays, he was always calm and gentle, not fast and brutal. Today must have been different.

"Bye," Luke said as he got out of the car, even though his dad was long gone. Luke didn't know why his father met with Dr. B every week, but he never really questioned it. Maybe it was something for school or for work. Luke didn't know. It didn't affect him, so he really didn't care. Besides, his dad seemed happy enough to go every week. Why would Luke stop him?

Luke's dad burst through the double doors on the corner of the building and ran to the hallway to where Dr. B's office was located in. His run turned into a walk as he got closer to Dr. B's office. The door was open. Luke's dad peaked through the doorway to see Dr. B's desk in the middle of the room facing the door. It had a lamp and a stack of papers on either side of it. In front of the desk were two plastic school chairs. Dr. B was in a nice office chair behind his desk, facing away from the door, staring out his window on his back wall. The lush-green trees were swaying their large leaves wherever the wind told them to. The chair Dr. B was sitting in was a nice shiny brown leather and had gold-colored buttons running down its sides.

Luke's dad gulped. "Hey, Timy," he said as he entered the room and sat down.

"Edward," Dr. B said. Dr. Timy Ballsadobe was balding. He had short brown hair that was about five inches away from his eyelashes.

"Sorry, I was late. I overslept—"

"I found it," Dr. B said calmly as he turned his chair to face Edward. "It was right under our noses this entire time!"

Edward's eyes widened. "Timy," he struggled to find the right words to say, "it's been fifty years. We don't even know if we're close."

"Yes, we do, Ed! You and I both know where close to the Prime World! It says Three on the portal. Ed, two more hops, and we are in paradise!" Dr. B said.

Edward put his hand on his forehead and sighed. "Supposed paradise, and Tim, we have been on this world for over half a century. I'VE moved on. I-I have a family. I have a son."

"A family!" Dr. B chuckled. "Your wife left you, and your son envies you, Ed! These people don't matter. This PLACE, it doesn't matter! The only thing that matters is getting to the Prime World. 'Supposed paradise?' No, it is paradise, Ed, and I know you once believed that too!"

Edward looked at Tim. Edward and Dr. B used to be brothers way back when. Maybe that's what Edward writes about in his journal. Maybe not? It didn't matter. After all these years, all Edward still saw was his brother, not by blood but by love. The man he spent his life on an adventure with had become *this* pessimistic, *this* nihilistic. It hurt Edward to his core. "PEOPLE matter. If you make them matter, Tim," Edward said somberly.

The school bell rang, breaking Edward's stare at Dr. B. Edward got up from his seat and said, "I'm sorry, Tim, but I'm staying here. I'm done chasing something I'm never going to find. I suggest you do the same. Besides, just because you and your sick cult believe it's going to be one thing doesn't mean it won't be another." Edward started to walk out of the room.

"Oh, that's what this is about!" Dr. B said, his brow starting to furrow. "You're just mad because you think I replaced you!"

Edward stayed silent, shaking his head as he started to shut the door behind him.

Dr. B shot up and bolted to the door, grabbing it before Edward could shut it. Dr. B yanked the door back open as Edward continued down the hall. "Don't you walk away from me!" Dr. B yelled. "How dare you walk away from me! How dare you walk away from OUR DREAM! What do you want to do, Edward?"

Edward kept walking.

"Die alone on this meaningless rock?" Dr. B shouted the question down the hall but got no answer. With Dr. B's face red and his brow fully furrowed, he slammed the door shut.

Dr. B stormed over to his desk and picked up his phone. He tapped on it a few times, and ringing started to play. Suddenly, a "Yes sir?" came out of the phone.

"Give me some good news," Dr. B said.

"The attack will be ready in the next week, sir. We get through this, and the Prime World is as good as ours, sir."

Dr. B took a long deep sigh. "Thank you," he said.

"Of course, sir."

Dr. B cracked a smile for half a second before hanging up the phone. He sat in his fancy seat and looked blankly at the closed door in front of him. His knee was bouncing up and down. His eye twitched, and he slammed his fist onto his desk. Then he slammed his fist into the stack of papers, knocking them over and watching as they float onto the ground. "Dammit, Ed!" He shouted into the empty room. *Whatever, I don't need him anyways*, he thought. He sighed, and his face fell into the palm of his hands.

CHAPTER 2

The Boys

Ten minutes earlier

Edward put the car in park and yanked the keys out of the ignition. "Bye!" he said abruptly as he opened his door, slammed it shut, and sprinted toward the back of the building.

"Bye," Luke said as he got out of the car. Luke saw his dad burst through the double doors on the side of the building. Luke didn't follow. As he got out of the car, he looked over at his friends' cars. The red truck was Logan's, who also brought Annie to school. There was the black car owned by Mike, who usually brought Preston to school. Next to Mike's car was Aidan's, and next to Aidan's was a car Logan had never seen before. It was a light-blue Volkswagen. A parking permit was at the bottom right of the windshield, and a little black tree hung from the rearview mirror. He brushed the thought off, excusing it as some random student's car, but deep down, he knew he recognized it.

He made his way toward the front of the building, and as he was walking on the sidewalk, he passed the *Shady Springs High School* sign that was to his right and walked past the busses that were dropping kids off to his left. All these kids walked to the main door of the school with their heads down while they either stared down at their phone or blasted music into their ears or both. Luke kept his head held high as he walked down the sidewalk.

Luke eventually made it through the main doors of the school and entered the supposed hellish landscape that is high school, *sup-*

posed being the keyword. Everybody at Shady Springs pretty much stayed in their own little group. Any stereotype you can think of was here. You had the drama kids, the football kids, the baseball kids, and, the worst of them all, the band kids. There were also the people that nobody talked about, the orchestra kids. They were all in their own little circle's talking among each other, although it sounded like they were all screaming at each other because of how loud it was in that main entrance the school staff liked to call the commons.

Luke was unfortunately a band kid, but he hated it. He hated the people in the band except for the occasional normal person like his friends Kody and Nate, although Luke only talks to them when he is in band class. He spent the rest of his time with the boys.

Speaking of, the boys always met right outside the new library located right through the commons and down a small flight of stairs. The boys met there every day before first period, and just like any other day, Luke walked over to the new library. The kids and school staff called this library the new library because it had been added to the building over the summer before the school year started.

Luke went down the stairs that led to the new library, and he saw them, the boys. There were six of them, Mike, Preston, Aidan, Logan, Annie, and, of course, Luke. They were standing in a circle, but Luke could immediately tell something was off—Annie wasn't there.

Luke joined the circle as Mike was talking. "So I got the first lump out, and then came a second lump immediately after. But get this, it gets stuck halfway out. So I make a mad effort to get it out. Eventually I do, but then a third lump gets stuck. I get that one out, and a fourth lump comes right out after but leaves behind tiny little nuggets that just wouldn't detach," one of Luke's friends, Mike, said to the group. Mike was a skinny nerd with slick black hair that was always combed and glasses that he had to wear all the time. Mike was also one of those orchestra kids we were talking about earlier. No one in the group said anything; they just looked at him blankly. "So that was my morning!" Mike added enthusiastically.

"And you wonder why we don't have girlfriends." Aidan added, shooting Logan a glance as he stepped aside to make more room for Luke who had joined the circle between him and Mike.

"Where's Annie?" Luke asked.

"I don't know," Logan, who was standing across from Luke, said. "She said she had to come to school early for some band thing, but that should have been over by now, right?" Logan added. Logan was a short but buff kid. He had curly brown hair and always wore shorts and a T-shirt, even in winter. Logan didn't do anything outside of school but smoke weed and drink till he passed out. He claims he isn't depressed or anything, just addicted. As the kids say, "Once you start, you can't stop."

"So she's still at the band thing," Aidan said, trying to dumb it down for Logan. Aidan was like Logan but a little more muscular. All he did was work out and play video games. He had black rimmed glasses and never ever touched weed or alcohol.

"Well, then why is Preston here?" Logan asked, trying to dumb it down for Aidan.

"Oh, I didn't have to go to that," Preston said in a gentle manner. Preston was a tall, handsome blonde beauty. His hair was like horses' mane, so majestic and alluring. He played the bassoon and carried the case every wear just to get a good workout in. Preston was also a very quiet individual, always observing but never engaging. Silent men, like Preston, are often thought to be wise, and the boys certainly believed Preston to be this way, but even fools are thought wise if they keep silent.

"So she is still there!" Aidan repeated, emphasizing every word.

"Luke, you see, this is why I don't like Aidan," Logan said.

"Hey, man, I never said I did either, and I think I saw her car here too." Luke added.

"The blue one?" Logan asked.

"Yeah."

"Yeah, that's hers." Preston added.

"Maybe she got sick?" Aidan assumed.

"People haven't gotten sick since the 2020s," Mike stated.

"And tell me, Mike, how much has changed in the past twenty years?" Aidan asked, turning toward Mike as he did so.

"Not much, surprisingly." Mike squinted his eyes as he realized in the past twenty years since the 2020s not much has really changed around the world. Its 2048, and the world is exactly like it was in the 2020s, despite some leaps in environmental sciences, although those leaps in environmental sciences didn't affect the boys too much, so they never really talked about it. At least, they thought it didn't affect them. The truth was with global warming out of the way, overpopulation slowly crept up as a threat.

"Wait, why would she be sick if her car is here?" Luke asked, thinking he missed something.

"Are you idiots?" Logan asked confidently. "She is obviously still at the band thing."

"I don't know," Mike said, "something about this doesn't sit right with me. I mean, humans haven't been sick in twenty years? That can't be right!"

"It is, but hey maybe you'll be the first person to get sick in the last twenty years?" Aidan added.

The bell rang, and suddenly a short, bald, angry kid ran across the room screaming. "I'm going into Penis World. Bye, Bye!"

The boys looked at each other, trying not to laugh. "If that's not a sign that today is going to be a good day, then I don't know what is," Mike said. The boys laughed and departed into their separate ways.

Luke's first hour was history with Mrs. Readsoft. Luke didn't like history. He thought it was pointless. *Mrs. Readsoft always says, "Those that fail to learn from history are doomed to repeat it."* Luke thought, *And she only says that because Winston Churchill said it a million years ago, but what are we learning from world history anyway? Not to start a mass genocide. Thanks, history class, now I know not to kill people—because I was totally going to do that before I took the class.* Anyway, Luke didn't like history, but that's okay because he did like his next class, statistics.

Luke didn't understand statistics, but at least it was interesting to him, and the teacher, Ms. Walls, was nice, which was an extra bonus. Annie was supposed to be in Luke's stats class, but she wasn't there. This was odd, given the fact that Annie hadn't missed a day of school since first grade. *Guess streaks don't last forever,* Luke thought. *She was probably just sick. Nope! That's not right. Her car was parked outside this morning.* Something was definitely wrong.

After class, Luke went up to Ms. Walls and said, "Annie wasn't here today."

"I saw," Ms. Walls said as she tightened some papers on her desk.

"I know, but her car was parked outside this morning. I think something might be wrong."

Ms. Walls stopped messing with the papers and looked directly at Luke with an ounce of worry and skepticism in her eye. "I'll send word to the office," she said.

Luke had noticed the hint of worry in her eye and recalled the memory as he left the room. Roaming the hall, all he could think about was the fact that Annie might be in some real trouble. If she was sick, that would be the first case in twenty years, but if she wasn't, then she was missing, and Luke didn't know which was worse.

Luke's next class was his favorite because he got to see his dad, Edward, in chemistry class. Edward was the chemistry teacher, and he was good at it too. Edward got his doctorate in chemistry from Harvard, and with all that knowledge, he decided to teach at his son's high school. Mike and Aidan were also in this class, and they hadn't seen Annie in their classes either. It was weird.

"Maybe she did get the flu?" Aidan spitballed. It was what flu season had been twenty years ago, so maybe it did make since.

"Yeah, but if she had the flu, then why did she go to the band thing?" Mike said.

"Maybe we'll see her in band next hour. Maybe she was just there all day," Luke said.

"I'm not in band," Mike said.

"Nor am I." Aidan added.

"Nor am I?" Mike asked, "What is this, the eighteen hundreds?"

"Right, sorry. Maybe I'll see her next hour."

"I just hope Logan's holding up all right," Aidan said. "You guys do know—"

"He likes her!" Luke and Mike said at the same time.

"I think everybody knows." Mike added.

"I just want to help him find the courage to ask her out already," Aidan said.

"I guess that can be scary," Luke said.

"Talking to women in general is scary." Mike added.

"Don't you talk to Annie all the time?" Luke asked.

"That is a purely platonic relationship," Mike said.

"You're not helping your case, pal." Aidan added.

Maybe I will see her next hour, Luke thought.

But when his next hour—that was band—came around, Annie was nowhere to be seen. Dr. B wasn't there either, weirdly enough. Dr. B was never late for class. He was the band teacher but stayed in his office on the phone the entire time. So he wasn't technically late per say. The students could see Dr. B on the phone, but he didn't care. Dr. B got up, still on the phone, walked over to his office door, waved his hands toward the kids as if he was trying to shoo away pigeons, and then proceeded to shut the door. All the students just sat there with their instruments on their lap, waiting for him. These were band kids; they didn't get on their phones; they just waited patiently for Dr. B to get off his.

Next to Luke sat Kody and Nate. Preston was also in this class but sat on the other side of the classroom in the front row with other people who played the same instrument. That's how the classroom was divided. You sit in the chairs arranged in an arch shape around the podium with the people who play the same instrument as you.

Kody, Nate, and Preston were Luke's friends, but they still didn't make a peep. Kody and Nate always confused Luke. You see, chemistry class was just down the hall from the band room. Kody and Nate's last class was on the opposite end of the school, yet every day, Kody and Nate got there before everyone else. Dr. B never seemed surprised. No one did, except for Luke. One day, Luke asked them, "How do you guys get to class so fast? Does your teacher let you out early or something?"

"No," Kody had said, "we just walk here."

"We know the shortcuts!" Nate added, nudging Luke on the shoulder.

Luke thought about that all the time. *Shortcuts? What does that even mean? Shady Springs High School was just hallways and big open commons. What shortcuts could they have taken?*

They waited for thirty minutes and sat silently, never making a peep. Finally, Dr. B emerged from his office and into the classroom. He had a clenched jaw, furrowed brows, and reddened skin. It looked like he might have had less hair than previously. Dr. B walked onto the stage area in front of the band kids and said, "Hello, everyone. My name is Dr. Timy Ballsabode. Go ahead, get it out of your system."

The kids giggled.

"But you can call me Dr. B. I don't know why I'm telling you this. It's the third week of school. You should know my name. Did you all practice like I told you to when I was on the phone?"

"You didn't tell us to do that though!" Kody said, speaking for the class.

"Yeah, you just waved your arm around before you shut your door." Nate added, trying to undercut Kody's remark.

"Oh, you stupid children!" Dr. B rubbed his forehead. He sighed and then said, "Those of you in the silver legion, practice is canceled after school today."

The silver legion was the name of the Shady Springs High School marching band. Most of the kids were awed and booed, but Luke, Kody, Nate, and Preston couldn't be happier, although that smile faded as Luke looked out at Annie's empty seat. Now, Luke was really worried. He could only imagine what Preston was thinking on the other side of the room. Now? Luke wasn't just worried but scared. He looked up at Dr. B, still standing at his podium, as a wave of possibilities rushed through his head.

Luke and Logan had their last three hours together: PE, anatomy, and ELA.

When Luke walked into the gym (where PE took place), he saw Logan pacing in the far corner. Everyone else in the class populated the other side of the gym, the side Luke had entered from and where Luke and Logan normally hung out at. Luke, while looking at Logan, tapped one of his classmates on the shoulder and asked, "What's up with him?" Luke had his suspicions, but he didn't think Annie's disappearance was affecting Logan *this* much.

Luke's classmate looked over, and Logan and shrugged. Luke sighed and started walking over to Logan. Logan, still pacing, noticed Luke approaching and froze up.

"Logan?"

Logan snapped out of it, twitching his head, and blinked fast and hard before saying, "Hey, Luke, what's up?"

"You okay?"

"Yeah, I—" He stared at the ground, his jaw slightly trembling, "She's not here," he stated. He shook his head and asked, "Why am I so worried?"

"Because you care, Logan. We all do. We're all worried about her, man."

Luke noticed Logan's hand shaking before Logan grabbed it with his other hand, "Then why aren't we doing anything about it? Why isn't anyone doing anything about it?"

"Hey," Luke grabbed Logan's shoulder, "I told Ms. Walls, all right? The office knows. They probably have the security guard looking for her as we speak."

"They should have the damn military looking for her!"

"Maybe they do, Logan," Luke said, not actually believing the military would be looking for her. "The point is it's out of our hands."

Logan didn't like that answer, but he knew it would have to suffice for now. Right now, his only goal was to get through the rest of the school day.

In Luke's next class, Luke and Logan didn't talk about Annie or the band. Luke just tried to cheer Logan up by making fun of each class they were in. Another one of Luke's and Logan's friends named Alex was in their anatomy class. Alex didn't hang out with the group outside of this class, much like Kody and Nate in band class. Alex was tall and skinny and was probably the best driver out of everyone in the school. In his free time, he would do street races to earn some extra cash. Alex didn't let a lot of people know that, but Luke and Logan knew.

"So there I was going ninety down highway 40," Alex said, "and this black truck is somehow keeping up with me. I look through my rear, and I see smoke start to come out of his hood."

"No way," Luke said.

Logan was looking straight ahead not at all listening to Alex's story.

"No way indeed," the anatomy teacher said as she passed back students' tests. She handed Alex his test. "Congratulations, Alex. You are the only kid in all my anatomy classes to get one hundred percent."

"I thought you said you didn't study?" Luke asked as the teacher gave Luke his test back.

"I didn't."

"I did, and I only got an eighty." Luke showed his score to Alex.

Alex chuckled and showed Luke his 100 percent while sticking his tongue out at him and blowing a raspberry.

Luke and Logan's last class was ELA, boring ELA where they did nothing of interest and were forced to read old books discussing philosophical ideas and political issues that the students had no interest in, including Luke and Logan. They barely talked and struggled to stay awake during this period. Well, Luke struggled to stay awake. Logan's mind was at much less ease.

Once the school day was over, the boys made their way back to their cars. Luke's dad usually had to stay late after school to finish his job and give extra help to students but not today. So Edward joined the boys on their way to their cars. They always parked right next to each other, in the top-right area of the parking lot, but when they got to their cars, the security guard was leaning on one of them waiting patiently for the boys.

"Are you guys friends with Annie Spilva?" the security guard asked.

CHAPTER 3

Detective Zack

Eight hours earlier

It was 7:00 a.m., and Luke was in his room, looking down, out the window, watching his bus drive right past his street. Luke turned around before he could see Zack in his truck, driving right behind the bus.

Zack was the new security guard for Shady Springs, only working for the school for about three weeks, enough time to get a good feel for the job. Zack was about thirty years old and skinny and had just a tad bit of muscle in his arms and legs, not a lot but enough to be noticeable through his uniform.

As Zack turned into the main road that led to the school, he studied the car in front of him. It looked like his father's, but it wasn't. Zack knew this because of the license plate. This car had a different set of numbers and letters. Then Zack started to think about his father. He thought about how much he had admired and trusted his father. He thought about how that trust scared him to death.

While Zack was approaching the stop sign that led into the school parking lot, the truck in front of him accelerated way past the speed limit and didn't even stop at the stop sign. It was a miracle that the truck didn't get hit. Zack did stop at the stop sign and waited for a car to pass, the car that could have hit that truck. Zack would have pulled that truck over, but he was just a security guard, not police. Zack proceeded to drive into the parking lot and parked his car as close to the school as he could get.

When he got out of the car, more of his uniform was revealed. His uniform was a typical security guard's uniform. It was black and blue with a gold badge on the corner of his chest. He had a black belt with a taser in its holster, a pepper spray in its holster, and some handcuffs in his back pocket. He made his way to the front entrance, passed the *Shady Springs High School* sign, and went through one of the side doors that led to the central office.

"Hey, Sally, is Principal Perry in his office?" Zack asked Sally, the secretary who was sitting behind her desk.

"Yeah, down the hall to the left." Sally the secretary pointed to her left, keeping her eyes on her computer screen as she let the rest of her sass out. "It'll be the first office you see."

"I know where his office is," Zack said calmly.

"Uh, huh," Sally said.

Principal Perry sent Zack a weird letter a couple of days earlier. The letter was for a new employment meeting. This was weird because Zack had already attended his new employment meeting, but the date on the letter was today, so here he was.

Zack went down the hallway. The walls were gray with mediocrity, and the floors were mundane. He turned left. The walls and floors were still the same, but there was this strange calm at the end of the hallway: a door, Principal Perry's door. Zack turned the knob and slowly opened the door. The lights were bright. Tall black metal cabinets were in each back corner of the office. In the middle was Principal Perry's wooden desk with a green lamp in the corner, with Principal Perry laying his head down on his desk. In front of his desk were two small leather chairs with glossy wooden arms.

As Principal Perry heard the creaks of the door, he slowly lifted his head. Seeing Zack entered the office, Principal Perry's head shot straight up.

"Detective Zack, please come in!" Principal Perry said in a hurry as he shuffled through yellow folders that were also on his desk.

Zack flicked the light switch, and the whole room lit up. Principal Perry squinted for a second before opening one of the yellow folders. "Perry, wh—"

"Take a seat detective, please." Principal Perry's voice was shaky as he pulled out a note card from the yellow folder and pushed it to the edge of his desk. Zack approached cautiously; he passed the seat, walked to the desk, and picked up the card. It was blank on the side facing up, so he flipped it over to see the words "Turn the lights out" written on it. Zack gave Principal Perry a puzzled look. "I just want to talk about how silly our names are." Principal Perry slid Zack another note card. Zack still looked confused but stayed silent as he read what was written on the other note card:

Eyes and ears everywhere.

Zack looked back up at Principal Perry, who was this time more scared than confused.

"I just find it so funny that my legal birthright name is Principal Perry and I'm an actual principal and your legal birthright name is Detective Zack and you're, well, you used to be an actual detective." Principal Perry's jaw trembled as he tried to sound as normal as possible.

Zack, also known as Detective Zack, could see the terror in Principle Perry's eyes.

"Yeah," Zack said as he slowly walked back to the door and flicked the light switch off. Principal Perry turned on his green lamp that sat in the corner of his desk. Zack walked back to the desk and was greeted by another note card. Zack grabbed it but didn't read it; instead, he sat down and asked, "Do you know who else might have…funny names?"

"I do!" This time, you could hear the shake in Principle Perry's voice as he shot the response out. A soft buzz sound came from the wall to the left of Principal Perry. Both he and Zack heard it, but neither of them looked over to investigate. "But I can't say." Principal Perry's eyes were wide open. "Principal-student confidentiality."

Zack finally looked down at the note card. This one wasn't a note. It was a name: Annie Spilva.

"You understand principal-student confidentiality?" Principal Perry asked.

"Yeah." Zack looked back down at the note card. He had a confused look on his face. He had never heard of an Annie Spilva before, and not to mention, the principal of the school gave him a bunch of note cards with words only a crazy person would write. The buzz from the wall, left of where Principal Perry was sitting, came back.

"Well, you better get going!" Principal Perry said as he shot up out of his seat.

Zack sat there still confused.

"You need to leave," Principal Perry said menacingly. He looked down at Zack with a furrowed brow.

Zack got up. "Well, thanks for having me," Zack said almost as if it was a question. He walked to the exit, flicked the lights back on, and opened the door. As soon as he walked out into the hallway, Mr. Willy bumped into him.

"Excuse me," Mr. Willy said, looking down at his phone. As he looked up and saw who he ran into, his plain expression turned into a menacing grin. "You have a lovely day," Mr. Willy said as he patted Zack on the back, walked into Principal Perry's office, and closed the door.

Zack looked down at the bottom of the door, waiting to see if the lights would go out. But they didn't. Zack looked back up at the wooden door. *Annie Spilva?* he thought. He walked back to the main office where Sally the secretary had been sitting still in front of a computer screen.

"Excuse me?" Zack leaned over the secretary's desk. "Can you look up a student for me?

Sally looked at him plainly. "Name?" she asked.

"Annie Spilva." Zack walked around the desk and leaned in next to her to get a better view of the screen. Sally took a quick confused glance at him as the computer loaded up Annie Spilva's profile. When it finally loaded, the letters *UEA* came up in the middle of her name and the number one.

"What does that mean?" Zack pointed to the *UEA* letters on the screen.

"Unexcused absence," Sally said. Not a moment later, the phone on Sally's desk rang. She picked it up and said, "Shady Springs High School, how can I help you?"

Zack stood up and turned his head to look around the room. He remembered what one of the note cards said, "Eyes and ears everywhere." He looked up at where the ceiling met the top corners of the walls to find a camera pointed right at him and the red light slowly blinking.

"All right thank you. You have a nice day!" Sally hung up the phone.

"Who was that?" Zack asked.

"Mr. Spilva calling to let us know"—she clicked on the UEA on the computer—"that Annie Spilva is sick and won't be coming into school today." Suddenly, with a few clicks, the UEA turned into an EA.

That doesn't make sense. Why would Principal Perry give Zack the name of a sick girl?

"When was the last time Annie missed school?" Zack asked.

Sally tapped on the keyboard. Clicks were the only noise in that room for a few minutes. Then the clicks stopped. She squinted, leaned in closer to the screen, and said, "Huh."

"What!"

"Annie hasn't missed a day of school since her kindergarten year."

"And now, after a decade, she suddenly starts missing school?"

"I mean it happens," Sally said. Zack agreed; it did happen. It was weird that after a decade, she got sick, but that does happen. If she is simply sick, then why did the principal give him a note card with her name on it? Being sick was a good explanation, but not good enough. He had to make sure. Then it dawned on him.

"Does she drive?" Zack asked.

"It says here she has a parking permit."

Zack grabbed a sticky note and a pen from the secretary's desk. "What's her number?" Zack asked. Each parking permit had a number so the teachers could tell whose car was whose if someone decided to park somewhere they weren't supposed to, like the teachers' parking or the handicap spots.

"256," she said. Zack wrote the number on the sticky note. "Her car won't be here. Her dad just called her in sick. It happens."

Zack ripped the sticky note out of the pad and walked to the office door. "I have to be sure." He sighed as he opened the door and walked out into the students' parking lot.

It took him an hour, going up and down row after row of parked cars, reading each and every number on each and every car parked in that parking lot, but he finally found it parked in the top-right corner of the parking lot, a light-blue Volkswagen with parking permit number 256. She was here. She wasn't sick. He looked around at the gray truck parked next to her car and at the streetlights all around the parking lot. He looked down the pole that held the streetlight up and saw a camera pointed right at Annie's car. He went back inside and into the security guard's office located in the school's main hallway, called the chicken walk, near the big gym on the far side of the school. He pulled the tape from that morning. The tape for today started at 4:00 a.m., no cars. He fast-forwarded to 5:00 a.m., and a flock of geese walked across the parking lot, but still no sign of Annie. Annie's car finally pulled in at 5:30 a.m., but then the tape froze on that screen. Zack squinted his eyes as the screen started to glitch out making weird static noises and the lights in his office started to flash on and off until suddenly all the screens shut off and all the lights went out.

"What the," Zack said under his breath as he left the lightless room and pulled out his walkie-talkie from his belt. "Hey," he said into the walkie-talkie, "can we get an IT guy down to the security guards' rooms? All the power just went out."

"I'll be there in a sec," a voice from the walkie-talkie said.

The IT guy spent the rest of the school day in that room, unable to get the power back on, and Zack did his normal security guard job for the rest of the school day. Just before the bell rang to end the school day, Zack went back outside and leaned on the hood of Annie's car. Zack didn't know much, but he knew Annie came to school today. He figured her friends might have parked next to her, and who better to interrogate than her friends?

CHAPTER 4

The Long Night

Once the school day was over, Edward and the boys made their way back to their cars. They always parked right next to each other, in the top-right area of the parking lot, but when they got to their cars, Zack was leaning on Annie's car.

"Are you guys friends with Annie Spilva?" Zack asked.

"Yeah, and that's her car you're leaning on!" Logan shouted.

Zack didn't move. "Do you know where she is?" Zack asked.

"She wasn't in class," Edward said, hugging his briefcase in his chest.

"She wasn't in any of our classes." Mike added.

"We thought she was just sick," Aidan said.

"Then why is her car here, dingus?" Mike slapped Aidan on the arm.

"That's a great question," Zack said, finally getting up off the car. He turned around to look at it. It was a light-blue Volkswagen. Her parking permit was at the bottom right of her windshield, and a little black tree hung from her rearview mirror.

"Wait, Logan, didn't you say she had to do some band thing?" Preston asked, lifting his bassoon up and down as if it were a dumbbell.

"Yeah, she texted me. Said she had some band rehearsal thing," Logan said.

Then why did her dad call her in sick? Zack thought, but he didn't ask. The less these kids knew, the better. Instead, Zack asked, "Can I see these texts?"

"Umm—" Logan paused for a moment. He didn't like people going through his phone, but as long as it's just the texts and as long as it helped find Annie, "Sure," Logan said. Logan whipped out his phone and held it up to where Zack couldn't see his screen as he scrolled to find the texts. Once he did, he turned his phone around so Zack could see them.

In the texts, Logan had asked, "Do you need me to bring you to school today?"

Annie responded with, "No, I got this band thing I have to go to at like five thirty this morning."

Zack looked over at Preston and his bassoon. "Did you go to this band thing?" Zack asked and handed Logan his phone back, who then turned his phone off and put in his pocket.

"I wasn't told to," Preston said.

"No one else from class had heard about this band thing either." Luke added.

"No one?" Zack asked. He kept his eyes on Preston. "Why not?"

"I think it was just a one-on-one thing," Preston said.

Zack's eyes narrowed. "You got a name, kid?"

"Preston."

"You got a last name, Preston?"

Preston cracked a smile. "Preston Dorris."

"Well, Mr. Dorris, which one of these is yours?" Zack waved his finger at the cars.

"None, my friend," Preston said. "I carpool with Mike."

Zack looked back at Annie's car. It was quiet. Zack's thoughts started to drift until Luke interfered.

"Is everything all right?" Luke asked.

"Is there anything you might need us to do?" Edward added.

"Everything's all right." Zack didn't know if that was a lie or the truth. "There is something you can do, go home. Don't go looking for your friend."

"She's not really my…friend," Edward said under his breath as Zack walked back toward the school and disappeared into the sea of cars trying to leave the parking lot.

The boys looked up at Edward with resentful expressions. "What?" Edward asked. "It's more of a student-teacher relationship."

Zack walked, at a somewhat quick pace, toward the back of the school where the band director Dr. B's office was located. Zack walked through the flood of kids trying to leave school. His walk was sluggish as if he was walking through mud, but he made it through. The farther into the school, the less kids there were. Zack was starting to freak out on the inside. As he walked down the hallway, toward Dr. B's office, all the possibilities of what could have happened to this girl started rushing through his head. What if she was raped or murdered or tortured or abducted by aliens? Zack's head always went to the worst possible scenarios when he didn't know what was going on. His hope was that when he talked to Dr. B, everything would make sense: the note cards with the principal and Annie's dad calling her in sick even though her car was at school, everything.

Zack finally made it to Dr. B's door and knocked. The force from his knock slowly opened the door with a soft squeak. Dr. B was in his chair, on the phone. He looked up at Zack and waved at him, signaling him to come in. Zack went in, closed the door behind him, and took a seat in one of the seats in front of Dr. B's desk.

"Yeah, yeah, hey, I'm going to have to call you back," Dr. B said. He had a snarky grin on his face as he hung up the phone. "Detective! Sorry, security guard Zack, what a pleasure it is to see you this afternoon." Dr. B stuck his hand out over his desk.

Zack grabbed it and shook it. "The pleasure is mine, Doctor. I'm sorry to interrupt your call."

"Oh, it's fine. Really. Just some personal loose ends I was tying up. How can I help you today, det, sorry, umm, Zack, is it?"

"My full name is Detective Zack. You can call me detective if you want. Um…so I was just checking with you. A student of yours by the name of Annie Spilva told some of her friends that she had a band rehearsal early this morning. She hasn't been seen since."

Dr. B's snarky grin faded as he heard the news. "I'm very sorry to hear that. I saw on my attendance that she was excused for the day, must have been sick or something. As for the band rehearsal thing,

I'm not aware of any band rehearsal this morning, at least I hope there wasn't because I wasn't there." Dr. B chuckled.

Zack stayed quiet before asking. "So you haven't seen her all day?"

Dr. B thought about this morning, throwing the girl into the blue portal, and then said, "No."

Someone was lying. Either Dr. B was lying to Detective Zack or Annie lied to her friends. Either way, Detective Zack now knew something for sure: Annie did not have a band rehearsal this morning.

"Well, if that's all, I actually do have to call that guy back," Dr. B said, pointing to the phone on his desk.

"Yes, of course, that will be all. You have a nice day, Dr. B," Zack said as he got up from his seat.

"You too," Dr. B said as his phone rang.

Zack left Dr. B's office and walked back out into the parking lot. The cars had cleared out by now. A few cars stayed in the parking lot, all the kids who had after-school activities, but Zack could easily see across the parking lot. He looked toward the top-right corner of the parking lot; Annie's car was still there but not the boys' cars.

He thought about what she said, band practice. Why would she tell Logan she had band practice and at five thirty in the morning? School didn't even start until seven. Why did her dad call her in sick?

He walked back to the front of the school and into the main office. Sally the secretary was standing by her desk, putting something Zack couldn't make out, into her purse.

"Can you do me a solid?" Zack asked as he walked around to the back of the desk.

"You caught me right in time. I was just about to turn off the computer," she said as she sat back down into her seat. "What do you need?"

"Can you give me the phone numbers to both of Annie Spilva's parents?"

"You're really worried about this Annie, aren't you?" she asked as she clacked away at the keyboard. "You know, this reminds me of that kid, a couple months ago, who didn't show up to school, and it turned out his whole family died in a massive car crash along with two other kids all from this school. I mean, what are the odds? Truly terrible. But tragedies like that are uncommon."

Knowing my luck, Zack thought.

The computer screen transformed from being a bunch of graphs to being a picture of Annie with blank graphs underneath her picture.

"That's weird," Sally said, leaning back in her chair and scratching her head.

"What?"

Sally sat back up in her seat. "Why wouldn't we—" She looked up at Detective Zack. "Nothing about her parents' information is in our records. No names, no phone numbers, nothing."

"Who would have the authority to change any of that?"

"Only Principal Perry, but—"

"Is he still in his office?" Zack asked as he started to walk down the hallway.

"No, he left during first hour. I haven't seen him since."

Zack stopped walking down the hallway and went back to the secretary's desk.

"What do you mean you haven't seen him since?" Zack asked.

"I'm saying he left during first hour, and he's been gone all day," Sally said.

"And you didn't think to tell anybody?"

"I didn't think to tell you! Besides, it's not a big deal," Sally said.

"You better hope it's not!" Now he had a missing student and a missing principle. Could this day get any better? Zack leaned down and reached over for a sticky note and a pen. *One problem at a time,* Zack thought. "Those kids you were talking about, the ones who were killed in the car accident? What were their names?" Zack asked.

"I only know the one, Ian Kelsay."

Zack wrote the name down on the sticky note. "Thank you," he said as he walked out of the main office and into the commons of the high school. He walked toward the west side of the school, went down a hallway and down some stairs, and turned left into the new library.

As he walked through the double-glass doors, he was greeted by the only other person in the library, the librarian. Lizzy the librarian sat at a wooden desk to the left of the entrance into the library. She had long dark-brown hair and black rimmed glasses. She sat at her desk, slouched down, staring into her bright-white computer screen. She didn't even notice Zack entering.

When Zack did enter, he immediately noticed how empty the library was. He knew school had ended, but he thought there would at least be some clubs meeting in this new giant library. Instead, there were empty hallways with walls made of shelves filled with books. Zack noticed some armless couches sat in the corner of the library. *No newspapers*, Zack thought. He walked back to the librarian's desk at the front of the library. He slammed his hands on the top of her desk and asked politely, "Do you guys have newspapers here?"

Lizzy the librarian steadily looked up at him, still slouching in her seat. She slowly started to smile as she studied Zacks expression, urgent and serious. That made it even funnier. Lizzy's smile turned into heaps of laughter as she finally leaned back in her seat. Zack could see tears falling down her cheek as she let out another roar of laughter.

Zack waited for the librarian to catch her breath. He didn't know what was so funny.

"Haha, I'm sorry that was…that was really good. 'Do you guys have newspapers here?'" She chuckled.

Zack still didn't get it. "Do you?"

The librarian chuckled again. She looked back up at Zack, his urgency turned to annoyance, and his seriousness turned to confusion. She stopped chuckling. "You're serious?"

"Yes, I'm serious. Do you have them or not?"

Another louder laugh came rushing out of her. "Dude, this is a high school library. No, we don't have newspapers." She wheezed. "There's a computer lab in the back." She got up and pointed to a room with a glass wall separating that room from the library. Zack could see old monitors stacked on even older computers. "What high-schooler wants to read the newspapers?" She laughed as Zack rolled his eyes and walked back into the computer lab.

Zack sat in one of the many empty chairs and turned on the computer. As the computer booted up, Zack brought out the sticky note with Ian Kelsay's name on it, out of his pocket. Once he was logged into the computer, he opened Google and typed "Kelsay car crash" into the search bar. He would have typed Ian Kelsay but didn't want to add unnecessary detail.

The first article that came up was one by Wolf Five news from three months ago. The headline read: "Three Shady Springs High School students died in a car crash off I-80." Zack scrolled down the article. Three students were involved, Ian Kalsey, Eli Peeling, and Dany Targen. Zack read the following paragraph: "All three students were part of the Shady Springs High School marching band entitled the Silver Legion."

Zack jumped up in his seat when Lizzy the librarian leaned through the doorframe of the computer lab and said, "I'm leaving. Turn everything off when you're done." She left before Zack could even respond.

He looked back at the computer, opened a new tab, and typed "Shady Springs High School missing students," but it was more of the same. All the articles he found were about the car crash three months ago, something that seemed to be public knowledge in this town. As he kept scrolling, he found a reddit post. Zack clicked it. The post's headline was: "All the missing kids from Shady Springs High School."

Zack scrolled down to find a PDF of a newspaper headline. Finally, newspapers. He found the one from three months ago, but as he kept scrolling, he found more. "Shady Springs student found dead," said a paper from six months ago. "2 Shady Springs students found dead this morning," said a paper from a year ago. Why hadn't Zack heard about these? He kept scrolling and found missing persons reports from friends and family. More and more students were dying, all attending this school. He kept reading. He kept scrolling. These missing persons reports date back to 1996, fifty-two years ago, fifty-two years of missing Shady Springs students. All are still missing and presumed dead to this day. Zack scrolled down a bit more; it was as much as the computer would let him. Below all the newspaper PDFs was a plain white text, which read, "The Silver Legion is coming."

Just as Zack read that, the power in the whole computer lab went out. His computer screen flashed black, and suddenly, the room fell silent. There were no fans or hums from the computer. Zack thought about the phrase again, *The Silver Legion is coming. The marching band? Where is the marching band going? And what does that have to do with all the missing students over the years?* Zack pulled his phone out of his pocket and read the time—12:47 a.m. It was midnight. He had spent his whole afternoon reading those articles, and he wasn't done.

Zack turned the flashlight on his phone on and walked out into the library. He figured that in the school library they might not have newspapers, but they would at least have the school yearbooks. He checked the librarian's desk and some random shelves before spotting the SSHS shelf right next to the back exit of the library. As he looked up the shelf, he found student-written novels and novellas, short stories, and poems. Then when he shined his phone's flashlight on the top shelf, he found it: the school yearbooks, dating back to 1962. He opened the newest yearbook, the one from this year. *The Silver Legion is coming* echoed through his mind as he flipped through the yearbook. He wanted to put faces to names. He flipped to Ian Kalsey, Eli Peeling, and Dany Targen, memorizing what they looked like. Ian had the face in the shape of a shovel. Eli was a white skinny boy with rectangular face, brown hair, and brown eyes. Dany had violet eyes, pale skin, and long pale-silver-gold hair. Zack flipped to the back of the yearbook. He looked at the Silver Legion's group panorama. Zack shined his phone flashlight on the page, squinted at the picture, and found them: Ian Kalsey, Eli Peeling, and Dany Targen. These kids weren't just Shady Springs High School members. They were part of the Shady Springs High School marching band. They were all part of the Silver Legion.

Zack got up and put the yearbooks back. He wanted to leave, go home, rest, and process all of this, but it was too much. He took a seat on the armless couch in the corner of the library. He yawned and thought, *I'll just take a quick nap.* But the moment he lay down, he was passed out on the couch.

CHAPTER 5

Alone and Dead

Ten hours earlier

"She's not really my…friend," Edward said under his breath as Zack walked back toward the school and disappeared into the sea of cars. The boys looked up at Edward with resentful expressions. "What?" Edward asked. "It's more of a student-teacher relationship."

"Okay." Preston scoffed.

"Guys, guess what!" Mike exclaimed.

"What?" Aidan asked.

"I took another poo!" Mike said.

"Nice, two in one day," Preston said.

"I know. I'm setting new standards in the pooping world. I mean, my shit looked like the most pristine piece of chalk in the world, perfectly symmetrical and cylindrical." Mike chef-kissed as he thought about his poo. "I should have taken a picture of it."

"No, you shouldn't," Aidan said.

"Thanks for telling us this, Mike," Logan said.

"Welp, I think it's time to go!" Edward exclaimed.

"Yep." Luke added as Edward and Luke turned and got into Edward's truck.

"Well, if they're leaving, Preston, you ready to go?" Mike asked. They always left at the same time.

"Yeah," Preston answered.

They got in their cars, leaving only Logan and Aidan. Aidan looked at both Edward and Mike's cars to make sure the doors were shut. Aidan nudged Logan on the shoulder as he asked, "So did you ask Annie out yet?"

Logan walked over to his big red truck, pulled the tailgate down, and hopped on top of it. "No," he said.

"Dang, I really thought you did. That's why I thought Annie was missing. She ran away after you asked her out."

Logan looked up at Aidan with a blank expression as Edward pulled out of his parking spot behind Aidan. Edward and Luke waved at Logan and Aidan, and Logan and Aidan waved back at them. Edward put the car in drive, and they drove into the line of cars, trying to leave the parking lot. Behind Logan, Mike and Preston pulled out of their parking spot, did not wave to Logan and Aidan, and drove into the line of cars, getting into the spot right behind Edward and Luke.

Aidan hopped on the tailgate and sat down next to Logan. Aidan was going to say something but didn't. They sat there and watched as the sea of cars flowed out of the parking lot, hundreds of kids on their way to continue their day. Logan and Aidan just watched. They didn't watch enviously or in resentment. They didn't really care. They just watched as if they were staring into the eye of nature itself, green trees in the distance and a blue sky in the background.

"What happened?" Aidan asked. "I thought you were going to ask her out after school yesterday once we all left?"

"I—" Logan thought about that moment yesterday, the nerves that had built up inside him, but he didn't want to tell Aidan that. He didn't want to tell anyone that. "It just didn't happen."

"Come on, man. You obviously like her. YOLO, bro, YOLO."

Logan had to think about the acronym for a second, YOLO, "You only live once." "You're right. You're right, next time I see her, I'll ask her out," he said.

"That's what you said last time."

Logan looked over at her empty car.

Aidan noticed his stare and sighed. "She's going to be okay, man."

Logan looked back up at the sky. "Whatever, bro." Logan pulled his phone out and checked the time. "Two thirty, I should probably go."

"Where are you going?" Aidan asked as he and Logan hopped off the tailgate.

Logan closed his tailgate and looked over at Aidan. "What do you think I'm going to do?"

"Get lung cancer."

Logan coughed. Aidan couldn't tell if it was real or fake. "Hell, yeah, I am bitch!" Logan said as he walked over and opened the door to his truck.

"All right, Walter White, I'll see you tomorrow," Aidan said as he got into his car parked two spots away from Logan's.

When Logan got in his car, the first thing he did was open his center console in the middle of his and the passenger's seat and take out an electric cigarette. He looked over at Annie's empty car through his window. He sighed. Regret. What do normal people do when they get this sad? Logan looked down at his electric cigarette. Do they talk to their friends or family? His friends he doesn't really talk to. His family he talks to even less. He put the cigarette in his mouth and inhaled sharply.

Logan turned on his radio, and music started blasting in the car. The bass from the song shook the car. He took another hit of his cigarette, put the car in reverse, backed out of his parking spot, and started driving down the road. He looked at the clock on his radio; it was two thirty-five.

Logan had texted his supplier they would meet up at two forty-five. That was the reason Logan didn't like people going through his phone. Most of his texts were his friends telling him whose house they were smoking at. If the security guard saw those when he was going through his phone, Logan and all his friends that he smoked with would have gotten in big trouble. Luckily, the security guard didn't see those texts. Normally, Logan would never let anyone go through his phone, but Annie was missing. She hadn't missed school in years, but now, out of the blue, she was missing.

Stop, he said in his head. He took another hit of his cig and pushed down harder on the gas pedal as he turned onto the main highway that went through the city of Shady Springs. He needed to get Annie off his mind, and the only way Logan knew how to do that was to get high.

Logan's smoking friends and his school friends (the boys) where completely different people. None of the other boys touched that stuff. The other boys knew the dangers of getting addicted to drugs, and that's not to say Logan didn't; he did. He knew better than anyone. He had witnessed that danger firsthand, but drugs are Logan's scapegoat, a way to relax when the pressures of the world got too high. Luke and Mike had video games. Preston had his music, and Aidan had church. Logan didn't believe in God, didn't play an instrument, and was terrible at video games. All the boys had their scapegoats, but the only thing that worked good enough for Logan was drugs.

Logan exited the highway and turned into a suburban neighborhood. In this neighborhood, the yards were bright green with sprinklers watering them. Logan parked in one of the houses' driveways, a house that looked exactly like every other house in that neighborhood, although Logan knew it wasn't like the other houses. This was the house his supplier stayed at.

Logan got out of his truck, climbed up the stairs, and entered the house. When Logan entered, he saw his smoking friends. Logan's smoking friends were your stereotypical drug addicts: skinny, tall, and dirt covering their skin. Logan didn't know their names. Well, he did, but he just didn't remember them. Their names didn't matter to him. They were the dealer and the two druggies to him. Those were all the names they needed.

The room they were in was dark. Soft light peered through the closed curtains covering the glass backdoor. The two druggies huddled in the corner. Trash and dirty clothes covered the floor. Logan looked further into the room. Logan saw the dealer where he always was, in front of the glass backdoor. Logan went to the dealer; he was the least skinny and dirty of the bunch and stood in front of a white foldable table that had rows of bags packed with white powder lined up in a very organized manner. These bags seemed to be the only thing organized in this entire house.

"You got it?" Logan asked, looking down at the ground, trying to avoid eye contact.

"How much?" the dealer asked.

Logan thought of Annie; that was the one thing he didn't want to do, and morphine was the only thing he could do to stop thinking of her. "I'll take double the usual," Logan said as he pulled his wallet out, took three hundred dollar bills out of his wallet, and placed it on the table.

The dealer grabbed the bills and put them somewhere under the table that Logan couldn't see. "Ten bags, of course," the dealer said elegantly as he grabbed the bags filled to the brim with a white powder and put them into a bigger plastic bag that looked like it had come from a supermarket. He lifted the bag, with both of his hands, over the table, and said, "Here you go, sir."

Logan snatched the bag as fast as a cheetah might snatch its dinner. He was about to leave when one of the addicts smoking in the corner of the room stopped him.

"Hey, hey, hey! Here." The addict handed Logan a long needle with some fluid in it. "Here, here, take this, man. It's way better than that white shit!" the addict spoke so jitterily yet calmly. "This shit will get your mind off of anything, man. I'm talking ANYTHING! Just stick it in, and all your problems will go away, man. All your problems just float away! A beautiful bliss!"

The addict threw the needle into Logan's bag, pulled another out of his pocket, and stuck it into his arm, an arm with multiple needle punctures already in it. Logan looked at the ground to see five or ten of those needles empty on the ground. Logan got out of the house before he could see the addict's reaction.

Logan got back into his red truck and threw the plastic bag into the passenger's seat as if he had just bought groceries from the supermarket. He looked over at the passenger's seat. Excluding the bag, the seat was empty. It didn't have to be. If he just had the courage to ask Annie out, she could be the one in that seat. Instead of going to buy drugs, he could have gone to a movie with her. She could be here with him. She could have been safe with him. Instead, she is missing, and nobody knows where she is, and for all anyone knows, she could be dead, alone and dead, just like him, all because of him!

At least that's how Logan saw it. He grabbed the needle out of the bag and jammed it into his arm. Suddenly, he felt as if he was floating in space. He put the car into drive and drove down the street, although it wasn't a street. He didn't just feel like he was floating in space, but he was in space, piloting a spaceship through an empty less void lit up by tiny dots arranged in no particular pattern.

Ahead of him, he could see a black hole. It got closer and closer as he accelerated in his spaceship. The black hole got bigger, closer, and darker, until it swallowed him whole. It was dark and silent except for what he could see inside his spaceship. So he got up, turned around, and entered the body of the ship, although it didn't look like the body of a ship. It just looked like a room. As he looked around, people he didn't even know started popping out of thin air, and these people started dancing.

Logan turned back around to where the pilot seat of his spaceship should have been, but it wasn't there. It was just more people dancing. All these people crammed into this foggy room like sardines in a tin can, everywhere except for where Logan stood.

It was as if a circular barrier forced all these people to stay about three feet away from him. Green and blue lights shot through the cloudy air, people were dancing with their arms in the air, and music was shaking the whole building. Logan was clueless in the middle of it.

Logan took a step forward, and suddenly, that barrier that kept all these people away gave way. These dancing people started closing in on him, like ants engulfing an abandoned piece of food on the ground. They swarmed and squished him, and he fell onto the ground. He felt as if he was getting swallowed whole as all these people surrounded him, stomped on him, and acted like he wasn't even there. As more and more people surrounded him, he started to see and hear less and less until nothing. He was back in that empty void of darkness. He felt like he was falling or flying; he couldn't tell.

He looked down or what he thought was down. A small light grew bigger and bigger as he got closer to it. As he got closer, the light turned out to be a room with no ceiling. That's how he saw inside as he continued to fall closer and closer to it. The room had a wooden floor and blank blue walls as he fell through where the ceiling should have been and plopped onto the floor.

The room was empty. As Logan sat up, he figured out what the room really was. It was his childhood bedroom. All the decorations and furniture had been removed, but it was his bedroom. He got up and turned around to find a teddy bear sitting up on the ground. It was his teddy bear from when he was younger.

The teddy bear looked up at him and said, "You must do the Harlem shake, Logan!" The teddy bear got up and walked over to a small plastic desk that materialized out of thin air. On top of this desk was a cup of water with a sock soaked in it. The teddy bear grabbed the cup of sock water and handed it to Logan. "Drink!" the teddy bear said.

Logan grabbed the cup but didn't drink it.

"Do you not want to see?" the teddy bear asked intellectually. The teddy bear walked over to Logan and tilted the cup into Logan's mouth, forcing the sock water into his mouth. Logan swallowed gulp after gulp, almost unconsciously. The more he swallowed, the more toys and furniture materialized into the room. His bed popped into the corner, posters populated the walls, and toys littered the ground.

One of the toys was a plastic plane that materialized right below his feet. Logan looked down at it, and before he knew it, he was in it, flying over a city, so close to the ground, he could see the detail in the old brick buildings. People were staring at him from the ground. As he looked around, he could see more noticeable buildings like the Empire State Building; in the distance, he could just make out the Flatiron Building, and as he looked in front of him, he saw a tower. He started to blink rapidly, and suddenly, everything made sense.

He wasn't in a plane; he was in his truck. He wasn't flying over a city; he was driving through his city, Shady Springs. In front of him wasn't a tower but a building: Shady Springs High School. For some reason, he decided to speed up as soon as he saw the building in front of him. He kept driving faster until *boom!*

He crashed into the side of the school. His truck was halfway through the school's front wall, and the bed of the truck stuck out on the outside of the school. Logan was passed out in his seat with his seat belt on and blood dripping down his face.

CHAPTER 6

The Car inside the Wall

Zack had awoken to the touch of a woman, something he hadn't felt in many moons. Lizzy the librarian was nudging him on the shoulder with her hand, trying to wake him up. He slowly opened his eyes to see the librarian's shocked expression and the fear in her eyes.

"Mmm…what happened?" Zack asked as he sat up on the couch, rubbing his eyes.

"You fell asleep on my couch as a student decided to crash into the front of the school," Lizzy the librarian said quick and sassy.

Zack's eyes widened, shocked by the news and still trying to wake up. "What!"

"Get up." Lizzy tugged on Zack's arm, trying to pull him out of the chair. "I can't believe you didn't even hear the crash."

Zack stood up with the librarian still pulling on his arm, leading him out of the library.

"The crash? What happened?" Zack asked, yanking his arm from the librarian's grip as they continued to walk down the hallway toward where the crash was located.

"I told you!" The librarian exclaimed. "A student got high and crashed into the school."

"Wait, wait, wait, wait. You didn't tell me this kid was high."

"Yeah, he was high and crashed into the school."

"Well, how do you know they were high?"

"Look, detective security guard, all your questions will be answered if you just come take a look."

Zack sighed as they continued walking down the school's hall-ways toward the crash. "It's too early for this. What time is it anyway?"

"Six thirty. Kids and teachers are going to start arriving here soon."

"Why are you here so early?" Zack asked.

"I live just down the street, heard the crash, and came rush-ing down. No one was there, so I called 911, but they still haven't arrived."

"No one was there?" Zack asked as they arrived at the door that led to the room the truck crashed into. The door that led to the room was in the middle of a hallway, right next to the men's bathroom door and across from the counseling office that had glass doors and walls looking out into the hallway.

"Take a look for yourself," the librarian said as she opened the door, next to the men's room, for Zack. The room was empty except for a few boxes along the side walls and stacked textbooks wrapped in saran wrap. The room was also dark, the only light peering through the giant hole in the wall. In the middle of that hole sat a big red truck with dents on its bumper and hood. The truck's front wind-shield and side windows were all shattered. Broken bricks from the school's wall lay on and around the red truck. Dust filled the room and got blown around from the wind rushing through the big hole in the wall.

Zack walked up to the truck. The hissing from the engine invaded Zack's eardrums as he walked to the truck's front door and peaked through the shattered window. The truck was empty, but he could see blood on the steering wheel and ziplock bags packed with white powder in the passenger's seat.

"You said you called the police, right?" Zack asked the librarian who was standing in the doorway, trying not to look at the wreck.

"Yeah, right before I found you."

Zack walked up to the hole in the wall and poked his head out. "Where are they?" Zack asked. He couldn't hear sirens and couldn't see flashing lights; there was nothing except for the cool morning breeze whisking onto his face.

"You said there was a kid in here." Zack turned back into the room to face the librarian and said, "I don't see any kid."

The librarian looked down at the floor as she said, "Well, I didn't exactly see anyone in the car."

"So it could have been anyone?" Zack asked as he turned back toward the hole in the wall. "And where are the cops?"

The librarian kept her head down. Zack started to pace back and forth. *Years of missing students, "The Silver Legion is coming," a truck crashing into a school, and no cops showing up. What is going on at this school?* Zack thought.

As Lizzy the librarian kept her head down, she started to notice something. She squinted her eyes to see drops of something red, but she couldn't make out what it was. She knelt down and said, "Zack, come take a look at this."

Zack stopped pacing, walked over to the librarian, and knelt down next to her. He immediately noticed the drops of what he assumed to be blood. He looked back at the truck as he remembered the blood on the stirring wheel. His head tilted as he followed the drops of blood from the truck to where he and the librarian knelt and out the room's door.

"He's still in the building!" Zack exclaimed before a giant steampunk woosh of an engine flew by the big hole in the wall, making them jump back up onto their feet. Zack quickly drifted over and peaked through the big hole in the wall. It was the school buses. Kids started to exit their buses, some of them started screaming, and as a collective group, they all started to run over to the crash site. More buses started to fill the parking lot, and more kids started to run over to the crash site.

Zack turned around. "Why does it seem like we are the only staff here? Where are the cops?" Zack shouted. "Call them again."

The librarian whipped out her phone. "It must really suck that you're the only security guard at this school huh?"

Zack gave her a pissed and annoyed look.

The librarian's phone rang. "There was no answer," the librarian said.

"No one answered your 911 call?" Zack massaged his head and then ran his hand through his hair. "What is going on?" he said under his breath.

Kids started to form around the truck and the hole in the wall. The librarian could hear footsteps coming from the hall. Zack could hear them too.

"Shit, shit, shit!" Zack said as he followed the blood trail out the door and into the hallway the kids were walking down. The kids ignorantly stepped into the blood trail and spread it all throughout the hallway.

"Well, there goes that lead," the librarian said calmly.

"Damn it!" Zack sighed. "Okay, you go to the main office, get custodians to block off this room, and keep the students from coming in from the outside. Get Principal Perry down here, and ask the secretary to call 911."

The librarian looked at Zack blankly.

"Go! I'll shut the door when you leave, and then I'll be in the front, keeping kids away from the truck."

"Okay, geez," the librarian said as she left the room and entered the steep stream of students.

Zack's eyes widened as he shut the door, turned around, went to the wall, shuffled in between the car and the wall, left the room, and went out of the school. Kids were still surrounding the crash site, screaming as if it was the most important thing in their lives. They took pictures and recorded videos of the aftermath.

"All right, everyone, it's time to go. Come on. Get to class!" Zack shouted into the sea of students. His voice was engulfed by the kids' screams, and none of them left. Zack sighed, looked over to his right, and saw three of the custodians shoving themselves through the students, trying to get to where Zack was. "Get to class!" Zack shouted again knowing no one was listening. He walked over to his right and told the custodians, who finally made it to where Zack was, to "make sure no one touches this truck!" The custodians nodded as Zack left the way they came.

Zack entered the main office to see Lizzy the librarian and Sally the secretary arguing.

"What do you mean 'they're not answering!'" Lizzy shouted.

"I mean exactly what I said. 911 didn't answer my call!" Sally exclaimed, standing up in front of her seat. Zack could see the frustration in her eyes.

"It's okay. They didn't answer us either," Zack said calmly. "Where's Perry?"

"He hasn't come in yet," Sally said as she sat down.

"Or maybe you just didn't see him come in," Zack noted. "Besides, don't you think it's weird he wasn't here yesterday either?"

Zack went down the mondain hallway that led to Principal Perry's office door. The door was shut. *Knock, knock.* No answer. He turned the doorknob slowly. The door creaked as it creeped open. The stench of rotting meat penetrated Zack's nose. Once the door was fully opened, Zack saw Principal Perry's head lying on the table with a bullet hole in his head and a gun in his left hand. The lamp on Principal Perry's desk was the only light illuminating the room. Flies buzzed around the dried blood that had gushed out of the hole in his head. Zack didn't move. The only noise was the flies buzzing around. Zack stood stationary as if there were two motionless corpses in that room, but Zack knew that wasn't true. He wasn't the one with a bullet in his head.

Zack's jaw trembled as he approached Perry's body. The flies buzzing got louder, and the stench of the rot penetrated densely into Zack's nostrils as he approached Perry. He looked over Perry's body. The dark-red dried blood bordering the walls of the wound seemed to go on endlessly through Perry's head. The light from the lamp on Perry's desk made the wound look glossier than it really was. Zack saw a fly fly into the hole in Perrys head, and Zack finally looked away. Zack's eyes followed Perry's arm down to Perry's hand that was holding the gun. Perry was grasping the gun as if he was about to shoot it, but Zack noticed something weird with Perry's index finger. It wasn't on the trigger; it was on the barrel, meaning Perry couldn't have shot himself. Someone else must have shot him. But who? Why? When?

Zack's jaw was still trembling as he quickly left the room, not touching anything, and went back to the secretary's desk at the front of the main office. Sally sat at her desk, typing something on her keyboard, while the librarian sat slouched in a chair against the wall to the left of the secretary's desk.

Zack whipped his phone out, pacing back and forth in front of the secretary's desk as he dialed 911. The line trilled for what felt to Zack like hours, but in reality, it was only about half a minute. No answer.

Sally looked at him, confused. The librarian sat up in her chair. Zack stopped pacing; not just his jaw but his whole body was trembling. Zack's hand that was holding his phone up to his face dropped down to his side as he looked down at the floor.

"What happened?" Sally asked.

Zack slowly looked up at her, still trembling. "You said you saw Perry leave."

Sally's eyes widened. "Yeah, why? Is he here?" she asked, starting to get up out of her seat.

"Stop!" Zack said. "Did you see Principal Perry himself leave yesterday morning?"

"I saw someone leave out of the corner of my eye. I assumed it was Principal Perry, but—" Sally's mind wandered off as she sat back down in her seat. "What happened to Perry?"

Zack ignored the question. "That guy I bumped into," Zack said as his body finally stopped trembling.

"What?" the librarian asked, leaning forward in her seat.

"Yesterday morning, after my meeting with Principal Perry, I bumped into someone as I left the room. I've seen him before through the school, but I don't know his na—"

"Zack!" Sally shouted with a tear falling down her cheek. "What happened to Perry?" she asked calmly, assuming the answer.

Zack's jaw started to tremble again. "He"—Zack took a deep breath—"he's dead."

CHAPTER 7

A Secretary's Scared Shouting

The librarian yelped, covering her mouth with her hand. Sally slowly closed her eyes as a second tear fell down her other cheek. Zack walked over to the librarian and sat down next to her. His knee started to relentlessly shake up and down. He could feel his heart pumping hard and fast inside his chest, chills creeping up his back. Zack thought about everything that rested on his shoulders, *Principal Perry's dead, Annie's missing along with a history of other missing students, the police still haven't shown up, and someone committed a hit and run into the front of the school. Oh, and you can't forget the Silver Legion is coming, whatever that means!*

Zack sighed deeply in through his nose and out through his mouth. The police weren't coming; he accepted that as fact. Zack knew that he alone would have to figure this out. The clacking of Sally's keyboard made Zack turn his head toward her.

Her brow furrowed as she looked at whatever was on her screen. The white light from the screen piercing onto her face as she said, "Zack, it doesn't say you were supposed to have a meeting with PP yesterday. No one was."

"I—"

"Which is weird because you were the only person, I recall, meeting him yesterday!"

"Were—"

"Which would make you the last person to see PP alive! Right?"

"But I wasn't!" Zack shot back. "If you would just let me talk for two seconds! I bumped into someone who works here in the band department. I've seen him help coach the marching band with Dr. B after school sometimes." Zack paused for a moment. "The Silver Legion," Zack whispered.

"Yeah, I know the name of our marching band!" Sally said.

Zack ignored her. "But I just don't know his name. Now, you might not have seen him come in because you were staring at your damn computer like your one of these ADD-filled, dumbass Gen Z students!" Zack reached into his pocket and pulled out the new employment letter Principal Perry had sent him and put it on the secretary's desk. That letter was the whole reason he showed up early yesterday.

Sally pulled the letter to her and read it in her head. "Your new employment thing was weeks ago."

"Read the date."

Her eyes glanced down the page. "Why would he…why wasn't I informed of this?"

"I don't think anyone was," Zack said, calming down. "He talked about our names but kept giving me note cards in the middle of the conversation. He told me to turn the lights out, which I did. He told me that there were eyes and ears everywhere and one that just said Annie Spilva. So I started looking into this Annie, and here we are. Something is going on at this school and," Zack pointed toward the wall that sat in front of Principal Perrys office. "I think Perry knew what that thing was, and I bet whoever I bumped into didn't want that thing to get leaked out to the public, and that's why they murdered Perry, to tie up loose ends."

"That's some real detective work," Lizzy the librarian said.

"That's some shit detective work," Sally said. "Sure, maybe I missed someone coming in and leaving, but that's a pretty big reach, and we still have a shit ton of problems on our hands—"

"It's a start," Zack said, cutting her off.

Lizzy looked up at the clock on the wall above Sally. "I need to get to the library. School's about to start."

"That's what you're worried about right now?" Zack asked. "We have a murder on campus and a truck lodged in the front of the school, and you're worried about the library? Nobody even goes in there!"

"Some students do!" Lizzy said defensively. "And the students and staff need to be informed about what happened to their principal."

"No, they don't!" Sally shouted.

"Not yet anyway." Zack added. "As a security guard here, I have no jurisdiction over a homicide on campus. That is Shady Springs Police Department's area of expertise. However, the person who crashed into the school is still in the building. We find them, and we can start getting some answers."

"Answers?" Lizzy asked.

"To Annie, to Perry, to everything. I mean you're telling me that all the tragedies of the past few days have been random? No way. All of this is connected. It has to be. I'm just not sure how yet."

Lizzy smiled. "So what should we do?"

"Sally, send out an email to all staff telling them to keep an eye out for any persons of interest. I'm talking bloody, bruised, maybe light-headed. After that, go on the intercom, and tell all the students to get to class immediately."

"Why not just say all that on the intercom?" Sally asked. "Wouldn't that be easier?"

"Easier? Yeah, but right now, the person who crashed into the school is not one hundred percent on any piece of information. They don't know we know they are in the building, and I want to keep in that way. Lizzy, you get students to their classes. I don't want anybody in the halls." Zack pointed to Sally. "You keep trying to get a hold of the cops. I don't know why they wouldn't be answering, while I go check in on the crash. Also, while I'm away, find pictures of all the staff that work with the marching band. I remember his face. I just need to know his name."

"I'd ask you to describe him, but I don't know any of those band losers," Lizzy said. "During the summer, I can hear them blaring their awful music. It's like, 'Can you please be quiet!'"

Zack and Sally looked at Lizzy blankly. Sally swallowed. "Yeah, I just know Dr. B."

"Me too," Zack said.

CHAPTER 8

The Pessimistic Perishing of Principal Perry

Twenty-four hours earlier

Zack got up from his chair in Principal Perry's office. "Well, thanks for having me," Zack said almost as if it was a question. He walked to the door, flicked the lights back on, and opened the door. As soon as he walked out into the hallway, Mr. Willy bumped into him.

"Excuse me," Mr. Willy said, looking down at his phone. As he looked up and saw who he ran into, his plain expression turned into a menacing grin. "You have a lovely day," Mr. Willy said as he patted Zack on the back, walked into Principal Perry's office, and closed the door.

Mr. Willy slowly locked the door and turned around to face Principal Perry, who was still sitting in his seat, stuffing a handkerchief into his side pocket. Mr. Willy smiled. "Did you have a nice chat with our new security guard friend?" Mr. Willy asked as he walked up to Principal Perry's desk and sat down in the same chair Zack had earlier.

"Ye...yes," Principal Perry anxiously spat out.

Mr. Willy leaned forward. "PP, I'm going to level with you. It... it hurts me to know what I have to do to you today."

"We just talked about our names!"

"How naive do you think we are?" Mr. Willy pointed to the wall where the buzzing noise had come from. "We have cameras in here. Yeah, you turned out the lights, but you kept the lamp on. We saw you give him something."

"It…it was papers. Documents for the job!"

"Stop," Mr. Willy said calmly, "stop lying, PP. Nothing you say can change my task here today." Mr. Willy reached into his pocket. "Dammit, Perry, we had a deal. You stay nice and quiet, you keep your mouth shut, and we keep our shit out of your school. That was the deal." Mr. Willy stood up, keeping his hand in his pocket, and walked next to Principal Perry. "But you couldn't even do that. Why, Perry? Why couldn't you just do that?"

Principal Perry kept looking forward as he answered, "I couldn't keep watching my students die."

"There not—" Mr. Willy sighed. "So is that what you told the security guard? That we're killing these kids?"

"No." Principal Perry's blank expression didn't move. "But he will find out, soon enough."

"Shit, Perry."

"I can't keep watching them die, Pat," Principal Perry said. (Mr. Willy's nickname was Pat.)

"Then you're going to hate what's coming." Mr. Willy pulled a gun, with a silencer attached, out of the pocket his hand was in, and shot principal Perry through the skull. Blood sprayed out the other side of his head, painting the walls with a splash of red. Principal Perry's lifeless head slammed onto the desk, making a louder noise than the bullet had two seconds earlier. Mr. Willy yanked the handkerchief out of Principal Perry's pocket, wiped his prints off the gun, and placed it in Principal Perry's hand that was lying across the desk.

Mr. Willy started to leave the office but stopped halfway. He turned around and looked back at the corpse he just created. *But I had to,* he told himself. He was just following orders, completing tasks to cross off a list, but he liked the list; he liked crossing tasks off. That feeling of completion and feeling of progress were enough for him. He turned around, unlocked the door, turned the lights out, and left the room, leaving nothing but a desk lamp illuminating Principal Perry's dead body.

As Mr. Willy left the main office through the front entrance of the school, Sally the secretary asked while staring at her computer, "How long will you be out PP?"

"Be back soon," Mr. Willy said, trying his hardest to sound like Principal Perry, and quickly left the main office.

Sally looked up from her desk, but Mr. Willy was already gone. She shrugged it off and went back to work.

Mr. Willy, now outside the school, started sprinting toward the back of the school, pulled the back double doors open, and rushed to Dr. B's office.

Dr. B was sipping coffee and turned around as Mr. Willy frantically entered his office. Dr. B checked him out, "Is it done?"

"He's dead, but we got bigger problems."

"Where is he?"

"We…we, wait, what?"

"Principal Perry? The body?"

"I…I framed it. I made it look like a suicide!"

Dr. B tightened his lips and forced a smile. "He's still in his office?"

"What did you want me to do, Tim? The secretary was right outside his office."

"You deal with it, Pat. That's the job." Dr. B put his coffee down and logged onto his computer.

"No, Tim. I signed up to be a band teacher, not a damn murderer."

Dr. B sighed. "Problems?"

"What?"

"You said we have problems."

"The security guard. Principal Perry said it's a matter of time before he figures out what we're doing."

Dr. B took a sip of his coffee and said, "Shit."

"We can't keep delaying the purge, Tim."

"We're not delaying. We're just not ready."

"Well, quite frankly, Doctor, we are running out of time. We do this now, or you can say goodbye to whatever is on the other side of that portal."

Dr. B looked up at Mr. Willy. "You realize I will have to be calling people all day. What am I supposed to do with the classes that I have to teach?"

"You deal with it, Tim. That's the damn job."

CHAPTER 9

The Purge

The next morning

It was 7:00 a.m., and Luke was in his room looking down, out the window, watching his bus drive right past his street like it did every morning, but this morning, Luke heard a helicopter woosh by his house going in the same direction the bus did. Luke thought little of it as he walked out of his room and into his dad's room to wake him up like he did every morning; however, this morning, Edward wasn't asleep. He was sitting upright in his bed, wearing the same clothes as yesterday, and clenching his journal in his lap.

"You're awake!" Luke chuckled.

Edward looked over at him, bags under his eyes, and tear stains down his cheek; then he slowly looked back down at his journal.

"Woah, hey, did you get any sleep last night?" Luke asked.

Edward said, "No."

"What? Why not?"

"I…I just…I can't. How did he? Why did he?" Edward looked back over at Luke who looked confused and scared for his dad. "Let's go," Edward said.

Luke, confused, furrowed his brow, but he went along with it. He knew his dad had terrible anxiety, but his journal helped him through it, his journal which he allowed nobody to read. The car ride to school that day was quiet. Some time on their way to school, Luke asked, "Do you want to talk about it?"

Edward said, "No."

"Can I read about it?" Luke asked, referring to Edward's journal.

"You know, Luke, someday, you are going to read that journal, and you're going to find out I'm not the man you think I am. Someday, you're going to find out…everything, but right now, I just need you to trust me, kid. Do you trust me?"

"Of course, I trust you, Dad."

Edward smiled. "Thank you, kid."

They continued to sit in silence until they drove by the school and saw the red truck crashed into the front of the building. "Is that Logan's truck?" Luke asked, to no response.

As they parked, Luke noticed Logan's truck wasn't there. Edward didn't seem to care as he left toward his classroom without even saying goodbye. As Luke walked into the school, he heard another helicopter woosh by and still thought nothing of it. Luke passed Logan's red truck while a crowd of people surrounded it. Luke glanced over the crowd and saw the custodians trying to escort people away from the crash.

Luke continued into the school, and as he approached the new library where the boys were, he noticed some of the boys were missing, not just Annie but Logan as well. "They're taking us out like flies," Luke said as he joined the conversation with Mike, Preston, and Aidan.

"Yeah, I know, dude." Mike chuckled.

"Luke, did you see the crash?" Aidan asked.

"Yeah, was that Logan's truck?" Luke asked.

"I think so. I mean, he's not here," Preston said.

"What do you think happened to him?" Luke asked.

"Same thing as Annie?" Aidan asked.

"I don't think so," Preston said.

"Which one of us is next?" Mike asked somberly.

Suddenly, the bell rang, making Mike clench his whole body. Not two seconds later, the intercom came on: "Attention! This is not a drill. We have a live shooter—"

Bang! Bang! Bang! Bang! Bang!

The intercom got cut off, but the boys could still hear the gunfire down the hall. Everyone immediately started to freak out, screaming and running. Luke started to frantically look around as the rest of the boys scream. "What do we do?"

"We stick together," Aidan answered as more gunfire could be heard down the hall toward the main entrance of the school.

Luke looked out the window that faces the dark morning outside the courtyard behind them. "Guys," Luke said as flashes of gunfire start to light up the courtyard and the sound of strafe grows louder and closer.

"In here!" Lizzy the librarian shouted behind them, freaking the boys out even more. She stood near the entrance to the new library, waving kids to enter. Kids immediately start to funnel their way into the new library, including the boys. Kids farther behind this funnel started to get shot from bullets coming down the hallway. "Quickly. Hurry the glass! It's bulletproof! They can't get us in here!" Lizzy said as she entered the funnel into the library. Kids started to rush in, tripping over other kids and leaving them to die. The boys managed to get in before a group of armed soldiers in black uniforms emerged from the hallway into the area outside the new library. These soldiers immediately started to rain fire into the remaining kids still outside the library. The librarian and some random kid shut and lock the library doors as they watched the soldiers outside finish the rest of the kids off. Most of the kids, including the librarian, started to catch their breath, right next to the glass doors, thinking they're safe. The boys, however, stuck together, went toward the back of the library, and ducked below bookshelves at the end of the row; that way, they can peek around and see what's going on. Conveniently, the row they chose to duck below was three rows away from the back exit of the library, a set of double wooden doors that led to a side hallway and more classrooms.

Aidan peeked around the bookshelf to see the soldiers—maybe ten or twenty—start to shoot the glass but stop a few seconds later once they realized it's bulletproof. Some of the kids standing next to the glass started to relax and even crack a smile, but most stayed anxious as one of the soldiers put the barrel of his AK an inch away from the glass and shot full auto until the glass shattered. This soldier's bullets started flying into the library and into most of the children who were standing next to the glass. Aidan turned back toward the boys to say, "We need to get out of here."

The soldier switched from full auto to semiauto to pick the rest of the students, to conserve ammo, one shot for one student. As the soldiers made their way through the library, they were calm and collected but also on guard and ready to pounce. They carefully walked down the library, each and every aisle one at a time, acting like they were military or as if they had done this a hundred times, holding their guns up, shooting any kid who got up and tried to run. Lucky for the boys, they didn't get up; they stayed ducked below the bookshelves as they quickly crawled over to the back exit of the library and quietly went through those double wooden doors, all without being seen by those soldiers.

"Holy shit," Preston said with a weird smile as he ran his hand through his hair.

There were two hallways: one went forward, and one ran parallel to the library and ran to its entrance. Luke looked up the hallway, where the entrance to the new library was, and saw glimpses of more soldiers running through the halls. Luke could see one of the soldiers had spotted them. "We gotta go!"

Luke grabbed Mike and yanked him into the hallway in front of them as the soldiers started to shoot in their direction. The boys ran down the hall, hearing the stomps of soldiers get closer to the intersection between the two halls. The boys made it to the end of the hallway. To the left is a door, and to the right is more hallway leading toward the courtyard. The boys turned left and started to push the doors open but instead just ran into them.

"What the hell?" Luke said as he continued to push on the door.

"Maybe it's a pull?" Mike said, trying to pull the door open.

"It's not a pull, dipshit. Why the hell are the doors locked?" Aidan asked.

Luke peeked down the hallway to see the two soldiers gaining on them. "I don't know, but we gotta go!"

Luke walked back, took a few deep breaths, and started sprinting up the hall that led to the courtyard. Gunshots followed as he sprinted past the first intersection from the hallway they just came down. Luke assumed the rest of the boys were behind him but didn't look back to confirm that assumption. Ahead was another intersection, a path left, right, and forward. Luke slowed down, looked both left and right to see more soldiers on each side, and decided to go forward into the courtyard.

As Luke anxiously pushed the double doors open that led to the courtyard, its small bright-green hills calmed him for a moment before a kid falling face-first into the concrete path in front of him brought him back to reality. The concrete path branched off and led to every other exit in the courtyard.

It was like they were trying to go through a wave crashing onto them from their side, kids running from the right to the left of the courtyard and soldiers gunning them down from the left. Luke tried to run through the middle as kids cut him off, bullets zipped right by him, and a helicopter swooped down right above him. Luke tried using his arm as a shield for his head as he sprinted across the court-yard, assuming the boys were behind him.

As Luke pulled open the double doors that led inside, he was presented with two more paths, forward or right. A flood of kids was coming from the right and heading forward. A group of soldiers were behind the flood from the right, mowing them down. So Luke went forward using people as cover and ducking below them to slide ahead. More kids poured into this flood from hallways to the right, but Luke continued to swiftly zip past them. He did this until he made it to the school's big main hallway that the kids liked to call the chicken walk.

The flood of kids appeared to be heading west or right through the chicken walk toward the parking lot. But if the exit doors aren't open near the library, why would they be open here? Luke knew his PE class was located in the gym on the other side of the chicken walk. He crossed the chicken walk, still assuming the boys were behind him, and turned left, heading south down a hallway that led to the big gym. He opened the big gym doors and walked into what looked like a makeshift medical bay, like something you would find during a war: kids and teachers packing the gym and no soldiers to be seen anywhere. Students and teachers who were injured lay in makeshift beds, the anatomy, health, and science teachers aiding them. A set of teachers watched over them from the balcony on the side of the gym.

Luke finally turned around to see if his friends were still behind him. Aidan and Preston were there, but wait, "Where's Mike?" he asked.

CHAPTER 10

Shitting in the Vape Room

Fifteen minutes earlier

"I'd ask you to describe him, but I don't know any of those band losers," Lizzy said. "During the summer, I can hear them blaring their awful music. It's like, 'Can you please be quiet!'"

They looked at Lizzy blankly. Sally swallowed. "Yeah, I just know Dr. B."

"Me too," Zack said.

They sat in awkward silence for a moment before the librarian blurted out, "Welp, I'm going to go," and proceeded to leave the main office, leaving Detective Zack and Sally.

Zack looked down at the floor, about to leave, but stopped and said, "I'm sorry."

Sally kept her eyes on the computer. "Just go."

Zack sighed, stumbled out of the office, and wandered down to the crash site. As he was walking, the stress of everything that was going on started to bubble up inside him again. Three weeks he's had this job, and in that short amount of time, a kid goes missing, another kid crashes into the school, and the principal gets murdered, all because of him. It's his job to secure this school, and he failed.

Right as Zack passed the men's restroom next to the crash site room, the bell rang, and the intercom came on: "Attention! This is not a drill. We have a live shooter—"

Bang! Bang! Bang! Bang! Bang!

Zack could hear the bangs, not just through the intercom but down the hall where he had just came from. As if it were muscle memory, Zack slid into the men's bathroom, slammed the door shut, and locked it in a matter of seconds. The gunfire grew louder, and as Zack slowly stepped away from the door, kids' screams could be heard echoing through the halls.

Zack turned his head toward the main part of the bathroom; he couldn't see anyone, but both the stall doors were shut. He pulled out his phone to try and call the police or really anyone since the police didn't seem like they wanted to answer that morning, but there were zero bars, no service. Usually, his phone would automatically connect to the school's Wi-Fi, but this time, it didn't, and when he tried to connect to the Wi-Fi, it didn't work.

Zack yanked out his walkie-talkie (thought I was going to write something else, didn't you) and said, "This is Detective Zack, does anyone copy? Over." He waited for a few seconds for an answer that would never be. He tried again, squeezing the walkie-talkie even harder this time. "This is security guard of Shady Springs High School, Detective Zack, does anyone copy? Over." Still there was no answer. "Anyone?" He stopped squeezing the walkie-talkie. "Please," he asked under his breath for an answer that would never be.

Zack started to tighten his lips as he walked over to one of the stall doors but screamed as he kicked the door open. "Shit!" He put the toilet seat's lid down, sat down, and stuffed his face in the palms of his hands with his fingers splayed as if grasping.

The question "are you shitting in the vape room, dawg?" made Zack jump out of his seat. The voice came from above; at first, Zack thought it was an angel, but then Zack looked up to see Logan perched over the stall wall with his head dangling over.

"You?" Zack recognized the face but couldn't remember the name. The name didn't matter though. Once Zack saw his face, he put the two pieces together instantly. "That's your truck in the room next door!" Zack got up and walked around to the other stall. Logan uncontrollably dropped back onto his toilet seat. Zack opened Logan's stall door to see white powder all over the floor and half-open baggies of the same white powder in the back of the stall. Zack also saw one of the ceiling tiles was on the ground right next to an empty box of cigarettes.

"That was an accident." Logan managed to mumble out. "I thought…I…I thought it was a different building."

Zack's jaw was practically on the ground. "I have so many questions," Zack said, "so you were going to crash into a different building? And why is the ceiling tile on the ground?" Zack started to pick up the ceiling tile, but Logan cut him off.

"No, no, no! I need it, man. It needsta! So it doesn't get all… all smokey!" Logan said, nodding his head. "And…and…and…and when there is no smokey," Logan whispered the next bit, "that way the security guard don't find's out about our smokey dokey, dawg."

"I am the security guard."

"Oh."

"And just because you took a ceiling tile out of the ceiling doesn't mean the smokes going to leave the bathroom, kid."

"Then where is it?"

"I—"

"See that's where you're wrong, Mr. bro cha cho guard. It's not the ceiling tile. It's the fire exit above it!"

Zack furrowed his brow. "Fire exit? There's no fire exit up there."

"Nah, man, its…its real. Like on the bus. The fire exit's on the ceiling of the bus. It's like one of them trapdoors!" Logan said.

"Yeah, I know what you're talking about, but why is there one on the roof of the school?"

"I know the answer," Logan said, holding up his finger, "so we can vape in the vape room! You see?" Logan pointed to his head. "I'm playing checkers. You're playing chess."

Zack chuckled, rolling his eyes. "Okay, man." Zack sat down on the floor. He couldn't hear the gunshots anymore. Zack saw Logan take a hit of his vape. "Hey, let me take a hit?" Zack asked, holding his hand out.

"Hell, yeah, man!" Logan tossed the vape to Zack. "We're in the fricking clouded up in here."

Zack took a hit of the vape and coughed it out almost immediately. "Watermelon? Really? What are you? Twelve?" Zack handed the vape back to Logan, who immediately took a hit.

They sat in silence for a moment. Logan kept taking hits of his vape, while Zack's mind started to wander. He kept thinking of the bell, the intercom, and the gunshots. "I killed that girl. I got her killed, and…and I…what is going on?"

Logan looked down at Zack, took another hit of his vape, and said, "I got my girl killed too."

"Annie?" Zack asked.

Logan sighed and took another hit of his vape.

"She's not dead, kid. I'm going to find her." Zack reassured him.

"In the vape room? I don't know, man. I'm starting to think girls…they're not even real. They're just…they're just in our heads, man. We made them up, man. With our imagination, man. Our third eye, man."

"Girls are real, kid. At least I hope they are. I mean if girls are a figment of my imagination, then I hate myself more than I realize."

"I ate an apple. I ate a grape. I was raped."

"What?"

Bang! Bang! Bang! Someone was slamming on the men's restroom door.

"Oh, shit," Zack said.

"Shoot them!" Logan screamed.

"I don't have a gun." All Zack had on him was a taser, a pepper spray, and some handcuffs, the same equipment he had on him every day. "What do you want me to do? Taser them?" Zack looked around, but the only door to this restroom was the one being banged on. Then he looked back in Logan's stall, the ceiling tile on the ground. Then he looked up at the missing ceiling tile in the ceiling and said, "You better be right about that trapdoor, kid."

Logan put the vape in his pocket and said, "Follow me." Logan climbed up onto the toilet seat, grabbed the stall wall, and lifted himself up into the hole in the ceiling.

From the ground, Zack saw Logan disappear into the ceiling. The banging on the restroom door stopped but quickly turned to gunfire. Zack quickly followed in Logan's footsteps until he was in the ceiling sandwiched between the ceiling tiles—somehow supporting his weight—and the roof of the building. About a foot away was a trapdoor onto the roof. He crawled over, and Logan helped him up out of the ceiling and onto the roof.

From the roof, Zack could see it all: a helicopter whirling on the other side of the school, waves of kids trying to get across the courtyard, and endless soldiers mowing them down. Then Logan saw Luke emerge in the courtyard from the other side of the school.

"Luke, Luke!" Logan screamed, waving his arms in the air, trying to get Luke's attention but to no avail. Following Luke came Preston, Aidan, and, lastly, Mike.

"Holy shit, we need to get out of here!" Zack shrilled.

"My friends! They're down there!" Logan blurted out pointing to the courtyard, nowhere close to where Luke was.

But Zack spotted them nonetheless. "They're heading southeast. We can head to that real fire escape." He pointed to a real fire escape made out of bricks with a green metal door southeast of where they were. Nothing was blocking their path to this fire exit except the silver metal junction boxes scattered along the roof. The helicopter, on the other side of the school, started to move toward them. "And we'll use the junction boxes as cover. Run!"

They both started sprinting across the roof as the helicopter swooped through the courtyard, and the soldiers in the courtyard continued to shoot down the students. The helicopter swooped up above the school and landed behind Zack and Logan as they continued to sprint across the roof. Logan looked down at the courtyard to see Mike lying on the concrete path as if he had passed out. Logan didn't see any blood, but he did see a bullet fly right past *his* head. The sound of the gunshot must have blended in with the rest of the gunfire below. Logan jumped behind a junction box right next to him. Zack had already made it to the door. Zack used the metal door as cover and shouted to Logan, "Come on!"

Logan waited a few seconds for what he assumed to be a break in the fire and then sprinted to the door like there was no tomorrow. Bullets flew right behind him, and by some miracle, he made it through the door. The second he did, Zack slammed it shut.

"Come on!" Zack said as he started to run down the stairs. "We don't have long. If your friends were heading down here, they're probably going to the gym."

"Wait!" Logan said, but Zack was already down the stairs. "Shit." Logan followed Zack. They went down a couple flights of stairs until the first door they came across had the sign *Gym Second Floor* on it. Zack pushed the door open to see a couple teachers leaning on the railing of the balcony that looked out onto the rest of the gym. The teachers quickly looked back at him and gave a sigh of relief. Zack slowly walked up to the railing, slowly getting shown the hundreds of kids and teachers taking shelter, the hundreds of students and teachers he has to protect.

CHAPTER 11

The Prime World

Dr. B was walking down a dark brick hallway. Two soldiers, who looked like the same soldiers who were shooting up the school, marched next to him. The soldiers had their assault rifles, and Dr. B had his pistol. The hallway was dark, and the only light was coming from the dim yellow lights spared across the hallway. The bricks were old, almost rustic, and made up the floor, walls, and ceiling. The hallway was like a maze, and different paths sprawled off each other, but Dr. B seemed to know where he was going.

Eventually, Dr. B made it to an exit. It was a weirdly shaped door: metal, skinny, and tall. Dr. B went through it and emerged out of a school locker in a normal school hallway. He was on the science side of the school, and right across from him was a chemistry classroom, Edward's chemistry classroom. Edward's door was closed. Dr. B went up and tried to open it, but it was locked.

Dr. B took a few steps back to let one of the soldiers shoot the doorknob. Three simple shots, and Dr. B could clearly hear the sound of panic on the other side of that door. Dr. B walked back to the door and furiously kicked it open with as much force as he could exert.

The first thing Dr. B saw was Edward holding a textbook over his head, about to swing it, but stops himself and lowered it when he saw who it was. His old friend Dr. Timy Ballsabode.

Dr. B punched Edward square in the face, causing Edward to drop his textbook, stumble backward, and put both of his hands on his face. Dr. B pulled out his pistol and shot Edward right above the kneecap. The bullet made Edward scream in pain as he fell onto the floor, now clenching his leg. The shot caused a roar of screams to come out of the kids.

Dr. B gave the kids a side-eye. "Kill them," he told the soldiers. "With REAL bullets." He emphasized. A wave of gunshots followed, and the screams died down. Dr. B saw the terror in Edward's eyes as he crawled backward until his back met the side of his desk. "It's a little crude I'll admit," Dr. B said, following Edward, "the base violence necessary for change."

"What the hell, Tim." Edward wasn't asking a question. "You killed those kids!" He cried. "You killed my students!"

"I killed them?" Dr. B asked, furrowing his brow and pointing to himself, cocky like. "No, no, no, your choices or lack thereof killed these kids, Ed. If it weren't for you, these kids would be going off with the others."

"So this is you! The others? The other kids you murdered!"

"How ignorant are you, Ed?" Dr. B shot back. "Killing kids for sport? I'm not a monster."

"Then what the hell do you call that?" Edward tilted his head toward his class of corpses.

"A necessity! You cannot stay here, Ed, and if you're not willing to leave," Dr. B tilted his head, "then you have to die."

"What the actual shit, Tim!" Edward cried as he clenched his leg. "What is this?"

Dr. B looked down at the ground. "A mission."

"A mission?"

"I need an army."

"You have an army."

"No, not the silver legion. I need a disposable army."

"A disposable army? No, you need help."

"Why do you think I'm doing this?"

"Mental help, dipshit! You're insane!" Edward cried out, looking around his classroom, all the blood and chunks of meat that flew off the children's bodies. "I mean look at that! The horror! Tim, what does this have to do with that portal? If you found it, then just leave. I...I...I...I don't I...I don't understand why?" Edward's voice was shaky and stuttering. "Why…why…why do you feel the need to kill these kids? For…for…for what? Tim? Huh, for what? For pride?"

"Pride." Dr. B chuckled. He didn't feel like explaining it again. Like he said earlier, he wasn't killing all the kids, but of course, Edward didn't listen. Ever since they got to this *specific* Earth, Edward had stopped listening. *That* pissed Dr. B off. Ever since he met that stupid girl, the same girl he killed and mourned, it was all a distraction. From there end goal. Determination is what Edward had mistaken for pride. "Is that what you think of me now?" Dr. B asked, glancing back up at him. "We were…brothers once. We shared a vision, Ed, a dream of freedom, of survival. We traversed the multiverse together, as brothers, as one, the Prime World, the answer to all of our problems, our one true hope of survival." Dr. B shook his head. "Do you even remember?"

"Of course, I remember. But we have been here for over half a century. I'm old. I wanted a family—"

"A family that you killed." Dr. B interrupted.

Edward tightened his lips.

"After all the worlds we've been to, how can't you see it?" Dr. B asked. "These people don't matter. Nothing does, and once nothing matters, your wants, your desires, your happiness, it's the only thing that's important. It's the only thing that does matter. All these people are going to die nevertheless. Our only hope is the Prime World."

"You don't know that!" Edward wept.

"Yes, I do!" Dr. B screamed back in a deep, rough voice. "And you once did too! You're telling me after all that time we spent hopping from Earth to Earth, all that time for what? Nothing?" Dr. B's face started to get red as he furrowed his brow and clenched his face. "We were so damn close, Ed! We were two worlds away from the Prime World, and you gave up. For what, Ed? A stupid, worthless whore?" Tears started to roll down Dr. B's face.

Edward proceeded with caution but was fairly certain on how this conversation would end. And he accepted that. He shook his head gently as he said, "I didn't give up, Tim. I just stopped running, running from that fear of death."

"I'm not scared of death. I just want to be able to live my life."

"Then live it."

"You know what's coming."

"Then let it come. It's like you said, everyone is going to die. Maybe it's meant to be."

"No. That THING"—Tim pointed outside the classroom, shaking from fear of just the thought of this THING, a thing he couldn't describe, a thing he didn't understand—"is unnatural. It's not MEANT TO BE."

"All those are excuses, Tim, excuses to keep running. We've been here for over half a century. We wasted our twenties with this multiverse shit. But there is still time to live our lives. You can still change, Tim." Edward rolled his eyes and chuckled. "'The base violence necessary for change.' That's what you said," Edward painfully pointed around the room, "all of this is." Edward shut his eyes and leaned his head back as he continued. "It's ironic, honestly. Change. You haven't—"

Bang!

Dr. B stood there, arm extended, held down at an angle, gun pointed at his brother. Dr. B stood there staring at his brother. Edward was lying down. His eyes were shut. A bullet hole, in his forehead, let out a tear of blood dripping down his head.

"I'm sorry, brother," Dr. B said, putting his gun back in his holster, "but no loose ends." Dr. B turned to the soldiers, pulled a grenade off one of their belts, pulled the pin out of it, and said, "Just in case," as he threw it into the area where the students had been. The explosion went off a few seconds after they had left the classroom. None of them turned around as they returned to the hallway behind the locker.

CHAPTER 12

Reunion

In the gym, on the balcony, Logan shut the door behind him as he entered from the fire escape. He saw a foldable white plastic chair along the wall, grabbed it, and pinned it against the door to act as lock so those soldiers from the roof couldn't come in behind them. It might not work, but at least it was a precaution. Logan turned around and walked over to the balcony, glancing over the railing into the raging ocean of wounded and scared students. His eyes wandered the sea of students, glancing over them, until he found the boys on the left side of the gym. The second Logan saw the boys, he immediately went down the stairs without saying a word.

Zack stayed on the balcony, looking over the railing. His jaw was trembling. He ran his hand through his hair as he took a step back, overwhelmed by this new burden. Mrs. Walls, Luke's statistics teacher, stood next to Zack, observing his anxiety. Zack noticed Mrs. Walls's observation and scoffed. "I've been here for three weeks, and in that time, a student goes missing, the principal gets murdered, and half of the students are already dead." Zack walked back over and almost let his face collapse on the railing, but he caught it with his hands. "Ever since I joined my dad as a detective," Zack shook his head, "it's just been one bad thing after the next."

Mrs. Walls squinted but didn't turn her head toward him. "What do you mean?" she asked, looking out over the railing.

Zack got the impression she didn't really care, so he only told her part of the truth. "I don't know, sometimes, I just…I feel like I'm cursed, like I'm poison. Everything I touch is poison, and once that poison spreads, it kills whatever it's leached onto. That poison killed my dad, so I ran here. And now it's spreading…like a cancer…and killing everyone here." Zack looked out into the sea of kids, blankly this time.

Mrs. Walls took a few glances back over at Zack, wondering if he was done talking. "Well, when was the last time there was a terrorist attack on the school? You're just one guy."

Zack sighed and took a glance over at Mrs. Walls who was still looking over the railing. No eye contact, but what was he expecting? He hadn't given her any either.

He looked over and spotted Logan walking across the gym. Then the questions started to pop up inside his mind. Why are all the kids here? Why are the teachers here? And why are there no soldiers here? He would have asked Mrs. Walls, but he doubt she knew. "Umm, give me a minute, would you?" Zack asked as he started to stride down the stairs.

Zack was long gone when Mrs. Walls answered with an "Uh-huh."

As Logan was walking across the gym, Alex, from Logan's anatomy class, spotted him from behind. "Logan!" Alex shouted, waving his hands in the air.

Logan heard his name, stopped, and looked around to try and find who said it. He fully turned around twice before he spotted Alex waving his arms in the air.

"Holy shit," Logan said under his breath as he walked over to Alex, slithering his way through the crowd of kids. "You're alive!" was the first thing Logan told Alex.

"So are you!" Alex said with a smile.

"Come on. Luke's over here," Logan said as he continued to make his way to the boys.

The boys were huddled in a circle, so they didn't see Logan or Alex coming until they squeezed themselves in. Logan looked around and found Luke, Aidan, Preston, and two people he had never met before but no Mike and no Annie.

"Logan!" Luke cried. He noticed Alex but didn't say anything to him. "Mike…we…we…is he with you? He was right behind us! We—"

"He didn't make it." Logan shook his head.

Luke covered his mouth. You could hear the force of his palm onto his face.

"Oh my, I'm so sorry," one of the kids, Logan had not met, said.

"I'm sorry, but who are you two?" Logan asked, pointing to the two he didn't know. It was Kody and Nate, Luke and Preston's friends from band class.

Luke took a deep breath. "Right, Kody, Nate, that's Logan, Alex, and Aidan. Alex, that's Preston." Luke pointed to each person as he said their name. "Did you see what happened to Mike?" Luke asked Logan.

"He was shot," Logan said somberly, "in the courtyard."

"How did you know?" Luke asked.

"Wait, were you in the courtyard?" Preston asked, suspiciously.

"I saw it happen." Logan continued. "He was right behind you, and then he wasn't."

"Where were you?" Preston asked again, slightly more hostile this time.

"On the roof," Logan said bluntly.

"The roof?" Kody asked.

"Wait, the roof? Logan, how'd you get up there?" Alex asked, turning his head.

"Something about smoking in the vape room," Zack said emerging from behind Logan, who he now knew the name of, thanks to overhearing Alex. Though he didn't know Alex's name. When one door closes, another opens.

"Vape room?" Nate asked disgustingly.

"Shitting," Aidan said somberly, remembering Mike.

"It's a long story," Logan said.

"Do you guys know why everyone is here?" Zack asked.

"The teachers," Kody said.

"I'm sorry?" Zack asked.

"The teachers," Alex interrupted, "they…they told us to come in here. Said it would be safe."

Teachers! What teachers? Zack looked around. He really should have paid attention when the staff was introducing themselves to him. *Why would they tell the kids to come in here? That's practically asking to be killed.* Speaking of being killed, he asked, "Where are the soldiers?" Zack asked.

The group of boys gave each other confused looks. None of them knew.

"I don't know." Aidan admitted.

"Should we be here?" Alex asked.

Logan heard the faint hum of a helicopter above. Not to mention, from what Logan and Zack could tell, no one had opened the door where they had entered. Logan and Zack looked at each other.

Leading lamb to a slaughterhouse, "We need to get out of here," Zack said.

"Where are we going to go?" Aidan asked.

Kody looked over at Nate. "The tunnels?" Kody asked.

"The locker room!" Nate said.

Kody snapped his fingers and pointed at Nate.

There was a slight pause before everyone asked at the same time, "What?"

"Here, follow me," Nate said as he started to walk toward the locker room located below the balcony Zack and Logan had come from. "There are these tunnels beneath the school," Nate explained. "They've apparently been here forever, predating the school being built way back in the eighties."

"That was seventy years ago," Zack said.

"We know," Kody said. "Only band kids are supposed to know about it. So don't tell anyone!" Kody demanded.

"These tunnels are how band kids get to class so fast," Nate explained.

"So you guys are just super-nerds!" Logan exclaimed.

"Wait, why didn't I know about these tunnels?" Luke asked.

Nate and Kody looked at each other, but the loud roar of a helicopter above the building disrupted their thought process. Two loud *bangs* made Zack turn his head toward the two main entrances of the gym. The doors were being kicked down by soldiers. There were four doors to the gym, one in each corner. Each door had been knocked down, and soldiers flooded into the gym, unloading round after round into the hopeless and scared. It was a trap, and they fell for it like fools.

"Run," Zack said, though they already had been. They ran in an orderly fashion, one in front of the other, with Nate leading the way and Zack, making sure no one fell behind, at the end. They kept their heads down, and Zack studied the floor as they ran toward the locker room. The bullets started to litter the ground, but they looked off. Before they entered the locker room, Zack quickly grabbed a bullet off the ground and stuck it in his pocket.

Once they were in the locker room, Zack quickly studied the room; there were rows of red lockers against the wall with rows sprouting out of the wall as well. Zack also noticed a room, maybe an office, near where they had entered with a window looking out into the locker room and an exit at the other end of the room.

Nate ran ahead to one locker located attached to a wall in the middle of the locker room. Nate messed with the lock attached to it and opened the locker with a swift ease as if it was his locker. Once the locker was unlocked, he swung the door open and said, "In here!"

Kody immediately jumped through, followed by Preston, Nate, and a hesitant Logan and Aidan. Luke looked down the locker. Nate was right. It did look like a tunnel, but before Luke could go through, Zack heard the locker-room door open. Zack grabbed Alex and Luke, kicked the locker door shut, and yanked the two boys toward the back exit of the locker room. The gunfire started spraying at them, but they were already out the door.

The hallway they found themselves in was empty. All the soldiers must have been in the gym. The only way out of this hallway was past the gym and into the chicken walk. Zack signaled to Luke and Alex, with a set of hand motions, to follow him. Luke and Alex had no clue what his signals meant, but they followed him nonetheless.

They quietly snuck past the gym. The doors were still knocked down. The soldiers were still inside the gym, walking over corpses. It was a miracle no one saw Zack, Luke, and Alex sneak past the open doorways. Once they were past the gym, the soldiers from the locker room came out of the back exit, same as Zack Alex and Luke did. Zack, Alex, and Luke started sprinting and turned into the chicken walk before the soldiers could start shooting. They continued down the chicken walk, and Alex and Luke followed Zack into the security guard's office. They shut the door before the soldiers even made it to the chicken walk. The security guard's office door was made completely out of wood, but that didn't stop Zack from both hearing and seeing the soldiers run past the office.

Zack turned his head toward the computer screens. There was live feed from every security camera in the school. Each camera showed hundreds of corpses littering the school grounds.

CHAPTER 13

Lost

Logan, Aidan, Preston, Kody, and Nate were walking down a dark brick hallway. The hallway was so dark, the only light coming from the dangling dim yellow lights spared across the ceiling. Kody could barely see the wires connecting them all. The bricks were old, almost rustic, and made up the floor, walls, and ceiling. Nate led the way. Different paths broke off at, what Aidan assumed to be, random points in the hall, but Nate seemed to know where he was going. They walked in silence, a scared silence, if there was such a thing.

Logan had no idea where they were going. He started to wonder where they might have been going but quickly came to the conclusion that he didn't care. He just wanted to see Annie again. He didn't have to talk to her; he just wanted to see her, actually see her, not just the vision of her in his mind. That would be enough. Would it not? He thought it would, but what if that just makes it hurt more?

Maybe it's for the best just to move on, to try and forget about her, about them. What *them*? There was never a them. He was too chicken to make a *them*, too scared, too scared to lose the only true friend he had, the only person willing to put up with his shit. He knew his friends pitied him. The laughing stock of the group—that's what he was, the screwup, drowned in drugs and alcohol and throwing his future away. That's what his friends thought of him. They might not have said it, but Logan knew.

"You okay?" Aidan asked, politely.

Logan gave him a side-eye. "I'm fine," he said as he pulled out his vape from his pocket and took a hit. "What the hell is this place anyway?"

"A labyrinth," Preston said.

"Under the school." Nate added more optimistically. "We should be safe down here. Only band kids know about it."

"So don't tell anyone about this place!" Kody exclaimed.

"Did Luke know about it?" Logan asked.

"No," Preston said.

"Why not? He's in"—Logan turned to Aidan and whispered—"he's in band, right?"

"Dr. B didn't wa—" Kody started but got cut off.

"We'll burn that bridge when we come to it," Preston said menacingly, as if he was playing a game of chess no one else could see.

"What does that mean?" Aidan asked.

Preston ignored the question. "Mr. Nate, where are we going?"

"To the band room," Nate answered.

"We're going back up there?" Logan asked, terrified. He took another hit of his vape.

"Let me rephrase. We are going to the room underneath the band room," Nate rephrased.

"Maybe there will be more band kids there," Kody said.

"Maybe they'll know what the hell is going on," Logan said.

"You really like using that word, don't you!" Kody exclaimed.

"What word?" Logan asked.

"The H word." Kody observed arrogantly.

"Hell?"

"Yeah."

"What? Do you not like that word?"

"No."

Logan chuckled. "Oh, really? Well, given how today is going, I'll be seeing you in hell by the end of the damn day!" Logan took another hit.

Kody scoffed. "All right, you little prick."

"Hey!" Aidan interrupted.

But Kody kept going. "Ever since we got down here, you have been one giant negative nelly, smoking that cancer machine, moping around, and now using that very offensive slur."

"Shut up," Nate said quietly, not paying attention to the conversation but instead to something in front of him. They were getting close to the band room. It was one turn away. He heard voices. Maybe it was the band kids? No. They sounded too old to be band kids. Who could it be?

"You know you can take that offensive slur and shove it up your ass!" Logan yelled.

"Shut up!" Nate shouted. "We're not alone down here."

"I thought that was the point," Logan said quietly, before he heard it too faintly. There were voices coming from ahead. Nate put his index finger to his lips, signaling to the group to be quiet, and they did. They stopped walking and stood very still. Everyone except Nate stayed a reasonable distance away from the corner that revealed the room beneath the band room (the band room's basement, if you will). Nate tiptoed to the corner, taking each step carefully. The voices in the band room's basement grew louder and deeper. These definitely weren't kids.

Nate peaked around the corner to see soldiers, the same soldiers from above, relaxing in the band room's basement. The band room's basement was different from the halls in this labyrinth. It had the same walls, but the walls were covered with bookshelves, framed pictures, and paintings. Tables and chairs littered the ground. Nate even saw his favorite ping-pong table. The band-room basement was like the commons of a college dorm. The soldiers were acting like people. It was weird, as if they were in the rec room during their nine to five.

That relaxation didn't last long once one of the soldiers noticed Nate peeking around the corner. The soldier immediately pointed Nate out and yelled. "Get him!"

Nate quickly turned around and started sprinting back to his friends, yelling, "Run!" His friends just stood there until he ran past them saying, "They saw me!" His friends looked back at where he had come to see soldier after soldier sprinting toward them. They immediately followed Nate down the hallway, and they turned right before the soldiers could shoot. They ran right, left, right, and right again. They followed Nate, who wasn't sure where he was going. He just knew that he *was* going, and the only thought that rattled through his mind was to run. So that's what he did.

After a solid five minutes of mindless turns left and right, they finally stopped to catch their breath.

"How do they know about down here?" Preston asked.

"Maybe they followed the band kids down here," Aidan said.

"Maybe there with the band kids!" Logan exclaimed.

"Are you just an idiot?" Kody asked. Preston shot a glance at Kody as he asked this.

Logan ignored the question and took another hit of his vape. *I'm the idiot,* he thought, *you're the one in band.*

Preston sighed. "Where the hell are we now?"

"We're lost." Nate sighed.

CHAPTER 14

The Lies of Loyalty

Alex looked at the computer screens that covered the side wall of the security guard's office. He observed the screens but not for long. He tilted his head down, looking at his feet, willing to really look at anything as long as it wasn't those screens. All the dead scared him and awakened a feeling deep inside him, a feeling that had been long lost, until now.

Luke and Zack kept their eyes on the screens as if the images were hypnotizing them, and in a way, they were—the gore, the guilt.

"How could you?" Alex asked, still looking down at his feet.

"What?" Luke asked, finally pulling his eyes away from the screen.

"Not you. Him." Alex's eyes shot to Zack, who's eyes were now pulled off the screen. "You left all these people to die!" Alex pointed to the screens.

The room went quiet for a moment. Zack's eyes tilted down, his lips tightened, and his jaw trembled slightly. He looked back up at Alex. "Well, at least I saved your sorry ass," Zack said somberly.

Luke's eyes darted back and forth, from Alex to Zack and back to Alex again. They were both right, in a way. If Zack had not helped them in the gym, they would have joined that mountain of corpses. But Zack could have also helped that mountain of corpses. Maybe that mountain didn't have to be.

Alex chuckled. "Luke, can you believe this guy?" Alex asked, shaking his head.

Luke was about to answer, before his eyes caught something on one of the monitors. "Is this a live feed?" Luke asked.

"Yeah, obviously. Why?" Zack asked.

"How is that obvious?" Luke asked as he pointed to one of the screens. His finger touched a bunch of men in blue uniforms on top of the little hill right outside the front of the school. "Police." Behind the boys in blue were white police cars, but the red and blue lights weren't flashing, although Zack, Alex, and Luke didn't seem to notice that part.

"Holy shit!" Zack said, whipping out his walkie-talkie, remembering that his phone wasn't getting any bars and he couldn't make any calls. Zack pressed the talk button on the walkie-talkie and said into it, "This is Detective Zack, I'm the security guard for Shady Springs High School, requesting assistance. You guys need to get your asses in here. There was some kind of attack. They're mowing down the kids like they're nothing, and I'm the only thing close to an officer in this school. These soldiers are trained and heavily armed, and I don't even have a damn gun. Please get in here and help us." Zack looked at the screen, staring at the officers who appeared to just be standing there.

A few seconds later, "The doors are locked" buzzed out of the walkie-talkie. It was the officers. "Detective Zack, who is also a security guard, not sure if I heard that right, tell us your location, and we'll send an evac team to come and get you."

"How do they know the doors are locked?" Luke asked.

"Didn't they just get here? What took them so long?" Alex asked.

Zack, not into the walkie-talkie, said, "In emergency situations, the secretary is supposed to flip a switch that puts the whole building in lockdown. No one in, no one out."

"That's why we couldn't leave when we escaped the library," Luke said quietly.

"In order to get through any of those doors," Zack continued, "we would have to make it to the main office at the front of the building, which is all the way on the other side of the school. Not to mention the power would have to stay on until we got there."

"Welp, that's just great." Alex scoffed.

Luke squinted his eyes slightly at the police on the screen. *Why did they just get here? Why weren't they here this morning? This morning.* Luke looked over at Zack and said, "The doors aren't the only way out of here."

"What do you…oh." Zack squeezed on the walkie-talkie and said, "There is a hole near the main entrance of the school. The bed of a red truck is sticking out of it. Do you see it?"

"Yes," the walkie-talkie buzzed. "Where are you?"

"You can send men through there. I can meet you there. We can get the rest of these kids out of here," Zack said, sounding hopeful for once.

Then there was silence. It was a long ten seconds before the walkie talkie buzzed out. "We…can't. We're waiting for…military backup."

"Military?" Alex queried.

"Something's not right," Luke claimed.

Zack believed him. "Why weren't you here this morning?" he asked into the radio. Zack watched the police on the monitor. The silence was deafening, much longer than ten seconds this time. The policemen huddled around each other as if they were arguing. One of the policemen walked away from the crowd. It looked like he was on the phone. Zack immediately checked his phone, still no bars. He tried to make a call, but it didn't go through. "Can you guys make calls?" he asked Luke and Alex, but neither of them could. They all had zero service, zero bars.

"We didn't get a call," finally buzzed out of the walkie-talkie.

"That's horseshit," Zack said to himself, even though it was technically true. The police didn't get a call because the police didn't answer when Zack, Lizzy, or Sally tried calling 911 that morning.

"Detective Zack, where is your location?" The frustration could be heard in the policeman's voice as he spoke into the walkie-talkie.

"All of these kids are going to die if you don't get your asses in here now!" Zack shouted into the walkie-talkie.

Alex and Luke exchanged worried expressions.

"We can't," the policeman said.

"Like shit you can't! I see the whole damn police force out there just standing around like you got a bunch of sticks up your asses!"

Then there was radio silence.

"Cowards!" Zack screamed as he slammed the radio onto the desk, destroying the bottom of the radio.

Alex scoffed. Luke almost did but managed to keep it in. Alex looked back at the screens. He looked at the one screen that was monitoring the courtyard. His eyes followed a soldier as he walked to one of the dead kids lying on the grassy fields. The soldier picked the kid up, threw them on his shoulder, and carried them back where the soldier had come from. "What are they—" Alex trailed off under his breath.

Zack started to notice it as well, and the soldiers were not just doing this in the courtyard but all around the school. The whole upper right of the school was already cleared out, no more corpses. It was as if no one had been there at all, as if it was abandoned, no bloodstains, just abandoned backpacks and unorganized chairs. Zack pulled out the bullet that he grabbed from the gym and held it up in front of his face, squinting as he did so.

"What's that?" Alex asked.

"It's what the soldiers were shooting," Zack said.

"That doesn't look like a bullet," Luke said.

"That's why I grabbed it," Zack said. It was true. This bullet didn't look like your typical bullet. It was much lighter and had a tiny needle sticking out of it. Zack held it up to his ear and shook it. It made a sloshing sound. "It sounds like there's a liquid in here."

"Poison?" Alex asked.

"Why bother? Why not just use real bullets?" Zack asked.

"Poison would mean no blood. No blood means no blood-stains," Alex said.

"That's true, but what would be so bad about a mess? I mean, school shootings have been popping up like a plague across this country. People have seen the mess. Why would these terrorists care what the public sees? I don't know what these psychos are doing, but whatever is inside this bullet holds the key to figuring all of this out," Zack said.

"My dad," Luke said, "he's the chemistry teacher. If anyone can find out what that liquid is, it's him."

Zack pondered on the thought for a moment. He needed to find out what was inside this bullet, but he didn't want to put Luke and Alex into any more danger. Finally, Zack came up with a compromise and asked, "Where's his classroom?"

"Down the hall, away from the gym," Luke emphasized, "and then to the left."

"Room number?" Zack asked.

"Two o' nine."

"All right, you two stay here," Zack said.

Zack started to walk toward the door before Alex said, "Wait! We're going with you."

Zack scoffed. "Like hell you are."

"He's my dad," Luke declared.

"And he'll probably kill me if he found out I let his son follow me into a war zone!" Zack said.

Luke sighed and looked over at the computer screens again, observing the soldiers and their locations. "Look, most of the soldiers are in the gym and courtyard area. It should be a straight shot to my dad's classroom."

Zack looked at the screens, grunted, and then said, "Fine, but you do everything I say the second I say it. Do you understand?"

"Yeah," they both said at the same time.

Zack rolled his eyes, unconvinced, and said, "Let's go."

A smile grew on Luke's face. Zack led the way, carefully opening the door, peaking around the corners to make sure there were no soldiers, and exiting the office in a quick and quiet manner.

CHAPTER 15

Pensive Practicality

"So you two rode together to school every day?" Kody asked Logan as they followed Preston, Aidan, and Nate down the old brick tunnels under the school. They were talking about Annie. Logan used to drive Annie to and from school, despite the fact that she had her own car and could drive herself. Driving her to school was one of the few reasons he actually showed up.

"To and from school ALMOST every day," Logan answered, pensive.

"And you were still nervous to ask her out?" Kody asked.

"Yeah."

"Even though she had her own car?"

"Yeah."

"And could have driven herself to school?"

"Yeah."

"But instead chose to ride with you, every single day?"

"Pretty much, yeah."

"Oh, buddy." Kody chuckled but the faded rather quickly. This situation with Logan and Annie reminded him of his past relationship. It reminded him of what could have been. It reminded him of the regret. He wasn't chuckling anymore.

Aidan, who was directly in front of them, couldn't help but let out a light chuckle. Aidan took a glance behind him to see Logan's worried face. He slowed down to let Kody and Logan catch up with him, and once they did, he asked Kody, "Can you give us a minute?"

Kody looked at Logan and said, "Yeah."

"Hey." Aidan nudged Logan on the shoulder. "Too bad she isn't here. She could be your"—Aidan waved his hand in the air—"damsel in distress!"

Logan's expression didn't change. "I don't know." He sighed. "A part of me is kind of glad she isn't here, you know? I mean, all the shit that happened once she disappeared. All the shit that's happened today alone. A terrorist attack on our own school. Not to mention what happened to Mike."

Aidan's eyes shot to the ground.

"And some kid crashed into the side of the school!" Logan exclaimed.

"Wasn't that you?" Aidan asked.

Logan finally grew a slight grin. "Yeah." They both chuckled, but then Logan's grin faded again. "I just miss her," he said. "I miss those car rides to school. I miss driving her to school and complaining about school on our way home. She would go on about the mildest inconvenience, too much homework, terrible teachers, annoying classmates, and I would just listen and occasionally come in there with a funny remark just to hear her chuckle, see her smile. I always loved that smile because it made me smile."

They were quiet for a moment. Aidan didn't know what to say.

Logan pulled out his vape but didn't take a hit of it. Logan continued. "Before her, this used to bring me happiness. It brought me peaceful bliss on a silver platter." Logan dropped the vape as he kept walking. "But now, I know it just numbed the pain."

Aidan took it all in. Eventually he said the only thing he could think of. "She's going to be okay, Logan. We are going to find her."

We don't know that! Logan thought, but he didn't want to argue. Instead, he tried to change the subject. "Do you guys think conjoined twins have one butt hole or two?" Logan asked this very important question loudly so everyone could hear.

"What?" Aidan scoffed.

"Two because there's two of them," Preston said.

"Yeah, but they're conjoined. So that would make one cause there." Kody clapped his hands.

"Shut up," Nate said, earnestly. But like always, no one listened to him. He thought he saw something ahead. Lights, maybe?

"But this begs the question," Logan said.

"This conversation doesn't actually beg anything," Aidan said quickly.

"Is it considered incest if they make out?" Logan asked.

"Shut up!" Nate said, louder this time while also turning around. Everyone immediately stopped walking and talking. Once everyone was quiet, they could finally hear the voices up ahead, same place those weird lights were coming from. They all look at each other, confused.

"We should go check it out," Preston said.

"What if it's more of those soldiers?" Nate whispered, but Preston was already tiptoeing his way toward the lights and the voices. When Preston got to the corner, it was revealed that the path they were on was connected to a balcony overlooking this strange room. Preston looked back toward Nate and the others and signaled them to come to the corner. Everyone except Nate immediately did. Nate's lips tightened, and his eyes bulged out as he waved his arms in the air, only to reluctantly follow them to the corner.

Once Nate got to the corner, he noticed the balcony overlooking the strange room and felt a bit safer. But once he peaked around the corner, that safe feeling left as quickly as it came. On the wall adjacent to the corner they were peaking, there was a big blue circular portal with unreadable writing all along the edges, although Nate could barely make out a number 3 on the top of the portal's edge. Along all the other walls were piles of children stacking multiple feet into the air. The bodies made a tight swirling path from the blue portal to the entrance doorway of the room. Beyond the entrance of the room, Nate could make out stairs climbing upward. Nate could not see though where the stairs led.

As Nate's eyes followed the path, his eyes darted back up to the balcony, safe from all the horrors below. He looked across the balcony to see a set of stairs, but before Nate could point them out, Preston whispered, "Stairs," as he pointed across the balcony.

Before anyone could do anything, Preston started crawling across the balcony, hugging the wall, trying not to be seen. Everyone quickly followed, Nate, again, being the last. Once they made it across the balcony, Preston started running up the steps, as if he had done it a hundred times, but most people have climbed steps before. So maybe it wasn't that weird. The stairs were metal with a red border and cold and went up in a triangular pattern fully surrounded by a bleak-gray concrete wall. It was dark, except for the dim-yellow LED on every other step. As they climbed, they could see light piercing through a set of closed double doors above them. Preston was the first to make it to the top and waited on a small platform in front of the double doors for Aidan, Kody, Logan, and Nate to get up there with him.

Once they were all up there, Preston quickly opened the double doors. The outside light was blinding at first. All they could see was white, but as time's arrow marched on, their eyes adjusted. They saw the outside world, the clear blue skies, and the bright-green grass. They were at the front of the school, same place the main office was and same place Logan had crashed his truck. Logan's crashed truck was not even a hundred feet to their right.

Aidan was the first to notice the police up the hill on the main road. He started to laugh as he pointed to them and said, "Police!"

The police all looked at each other, confused.

"We made it!" Nate said.

One of the policemen took a few steps toward them.

"We're safe!" Kody laughed.

The policemen pulled out his pistol, aimed it at the kids, and started shooting. The first bang was earsplitting. That first bullet went right through Kody's forehead. Nate heard the sloosh as the bullet flew through Kody's brain. The blood ran down his face as if he was crying blood. He was still smiling as his body toppled to the ground and left a puddle of blood.

Preston started running toward the main entrance of the school. Nate grabbed Logan and Aidan by the shirt and started following Preston as two more shots went off, both of them flying over Kody's corpse.

Preston approached Logan's truck and the hole in the wall. He dived back into the school as a bullet dinked off the bed of the truck. Nate pushed Logan and pulled Aidan as all three of them squeezed in between the hole in the wall and the bed of Logan's truck.

They fell to the ground and lay there for a few peaceful seconds before another bang went off and one of the back windows on Logan's truck shattered. Logan quickly flopped back onto his own two feet and said, "Follow me." Nate, Aidan, and Preston quickly got up, looked at each other with surprised glances, and followed Logan.

Logan led them out of the truck room and into the bathroom next door, the same bathroom he hid in at the beginning of the day. They got in a circle, not on purpose but almost as instinct. They were all panting and looking at each other before Logan broke the silence. "We need to find Alex and Luke!"

CHAPTER 16

Like Father, Like Son

Zack, Luke, and Alex ran through the halls of the school with no trouble at all. Zack led the way, stopping and peaking around every corner to make sure there were no soldiers on the other side. Every time he peaked around those corners, he found no soldiers roaming the halls. Zack remembered what he saw on the security cameras: the soldiers picking up the bodies in the courtyard and around the gym. Those places were on the other side of the school, but not all the soldiers could be over there, could they?

They must have. The halls were so empty. It was like they were walking around the campus after everyone had went home for the day. It was like the end of a shift. It would have been around the end of Detective Zack's shift, had it been a normal day.

Luke watched from behind as Zack jogged over to Edward's classroom. Luke watched as Zack paused in the frame of the door as his expression died. Luke and Alex followed Zack into the frame of the door. The first and only thing Luke saw was Edward, his father, lying on the ground, backed up against his desk with a bullet hole in his head, a tear of dried blood falling down his face, his eyes shut, his mouth open, his arm resting on his stomach.

It was the only thing Luke could see, tunnel visioned, right in front of him, his father lying dead. Luke shoved Zack aside as he sprinted to his father, fell on his knees, and slid right up next to him. Luke grabbed his father's hand off his stomach and said, "Dad? Dad? Dad? Wake up, Dad! Please, Dad! Wake up!" Luke put his fingers up to his father's neck to check for a pulse, but there was none.

Zack covered his mouth with his hand. Alex tightly shut his eyes. But the smell of smoke made him open them again. To the left of Edward and Luke was even more horror: tables knocked over and flipped on their side and kids lying on the ground and against the tables, with holes in their bodies. Blood was squirted everywhere. The blood flooded the floors and splattered against the walls and cabinets. In the middle of that mayhem was a small fire, and around it were kids lying motionless with parts of their bodies blown off. One kid was missing an arm, another a leg. One kid had a side of his stomach blown out, guts pouring out.

Tears were falling down Luke's face as he rested his father's hand on his forehead. Luke's tears fell off his face and sunk into his father's shirt. Zack nudged Alex on the arm and pointed out a fire extinguisher on the other side of the classroom. Alex saw it and treaded carefully across the classroom, trying not to step on anybody. The fire extinguisher was protected by a thin piece of glass that Alex had to punch and shatter. He carefully grabbed the fire extinguisher, ran back to the middle of the classroom, and put the fire out.

Luke leaned back against the wall right next to him. He let go of his father's hand, letting it fall to the cold tile on the ground. Luke curled up into a ball and started bawling. Zack shut the door and walked over to Alex who was still in the middle of the room. Zack looked down at the bodies. "This is all kinds of messed up."

Alex was looking at Luke when he quietly asked Zack, "Should we talk to him?"

"What would you say?" Zack asked, picturing his father lying there instead of Luke's.

"I…don't…know," Alex said slowly, with a dead expression on his face.

Zack shook his head, snapping out of the illusion, the very illusion he had already witnessed because it wasn't an illusion at all; it was the past. Zack looked around, and behind him, he saw magnifier scopes lying on the counters. When he looked at the cabinets above, hanging on the wall, he found syringes and little glass trays. Zack handed Alex the bullet and said, "Find out what's in here. I'll go talk to Luke."

"Shouldn't I? I mean no offense, but I am his friend," Alex said.

Zack looked over at Edward's desk, and a journal sitting in the corner caught his eye. "I lost my dad too. I know how it feels."

Alex looked down, feeling bad that he offered. He took the bullet and walked to the back of the room.

Zack walked over to Edward's desk. A pile of papers and folders populated the sides of the desk, papers and folders that would never be looked at again. A laptop sat at the center of the desk. It was closed, and it would most likely stay that way forever. The journal was to the left of the closed laptop. Zack observed its leather exterior. His father kept a journal just like this. He thought about handing the journal to Luke but decided against it when he glanced over at Luke curled up in his ball. Zack treaded lightly toward Luke.

Luke heard him walking over. Luke sniffled and said, "Just give me a minute," as Zack proceeded to sit down right next to him, his back and head against the wall. Zack tilted his head up and stared at the white mundane ceiling. Luke started to say, "I said—" but got cut off.

"My dad died a couple of months ago. I know how it feels, kid. I'm sorry."

Luke stayed curled up in a ball.

"He's actually why I took this job. I just couldn't do it without him." Zack looked over at Luke. still curled up in a ball. Zack looked out into the classroom and let the memories wash over him. "Ever since I was a kid, I wanted to be just like my dad. He was my hero, a detective! A true detective! Solving mysteries, putting away bad guys. But it wasn't just being a detective that made him my hero. Everything he did made him my hero. He helped me when I crashed on my bike, when I fell off the swing, when I hurt myself, he patched me up. I remember we would do everything together, me and my old man." Zack chuckled as he remembered, "When I was a kid, we had a toy lawnmower, and I would follow him around as he cut the grass. I wanted to do everything with my dad, and that was the plan. He was a detective, so I trained day and night to be a detective. It didn't matter what my dad was or what he did, I would have followed him to the end of the earth had he went there, and he did, and I followed. We were detectives, partners. Like father, like son."

"That's nice," Luke said, peaking out of his ball.

"It was," Zack said. "After a couple months of us being partners, we get called out to this crime scene. The weird thing was once we got there, no one was there. No police, no-no nothing. My dad said we might have been early, whatever the hell that was supposed to mean. So we go out"—Zack replayed the memory in his head, reliving the dread before saying it—"and we started investigating." Zack gulped and sighed as he continued. "It was dark out. The rain was pouring. It was a metal barn. The noise could have been anything." Zack shot out. He went back to that feeling of dread as he continued. "My dad heard a noise and whipped out his gun, but a bullet flew out of the darkness and shot through his stomach. I pulled my gun out. I could hear the shooter running away. He clearly didn't mean to, but I killed him anyway."

Zack stared out, wide-eyed, "As my dad was lying there, bleeding out, he grabbed my hand, and I'll never forget what he told me that day. I'll never forget it, he said, 'Zack, there will be times in your life when you get lost. Zack, when you get lost, you run straight ahead, and you keep running, no matter what. There will be people in your life who will try and hold you back, slow you down, but you cannot let them. Don't you stop running, Zack, and don't you ever look behind you. All past is history.'"

A tear fell down Zack's cheek as he continued. "I quit the next day. It's funny. It seems like your whole life you want time to slow down. Then when it finally does, you just want it to go fast again." Zack sighed. "Those next few months were hell, but as I reflected, as I learned to live without my father, I gained something. One day, I was sitting there, meditating, and it just hit me like a ton of bricks, an ounce of knowledge that—along with my father's final words— changed my life forever. You see, Luke, after my father died, I sought out inner peace, and I found it, but it's not what they tell you it is. Inner peace is sadness, Luke. People say inner peace will make you happy. No. It will simply clear the mind. Once the mind is clear, you realize when someone is happy, someone else must be sad. True inner peace is sadness so that someone else can be happy.

"It isn't David versus Goliath. It is a pendulum, forever swaying back and forth. Happy or sad. And as you walk through life, Luke, you will find people in the middle of that pendulum. Neither happy nor sad. They're stationary. They're numb."

Luke emerged from his ball and looked over at Zack, who had multiple tears falling down his stone-cold blank face. He looked over at Luke, whipped the tears from his face, and looked up at Edward's desk. The journal partially hanging off the edge of the desk caught Zack's eye. "My father wrote in a journal. I never got to read it. I believe your father's journal is on his desk up there." Zack pointed up toward Edward's desk. "Thought maybe you'd want to read it." Zack got up off the ground and said, "I'll give you a minute." He paused before adding "I'm sorry" and then proceeded to walk over to Alex on the other side of the classroom.

CHAPTER 17

Edward's Journal

Luke looked up at his father's desk. He remembered some of his father's words: "You know Luke, someday, you are going to read that journal, and you're going to find out I'm not the man you think I am."

Luke leaned upward and grabbed the journal from his father's desk. *Then who were you?* Luke thought as he merged his legs into a cross-leg position. He gripped the journal with both of his hands. It's leather, mesmerizing. The journal sunk into Luke's hands as if it was a part of him because in a way, it was.

Luke looked at the journal and its blank cover. "Someday, you're going to find out…everything." He looked up at his father but just saw the body, and he couldn't take it. His head shot back down, and he opened the journal.

Earth-3
1996
52 Years Ago

I'm starting a new journal today because today Dr. B and I have arrived on Earth-3. Our companion from previous worlds, Barry White, did not join us into Earth 3 due to cosmic dilemmas that he chose to face, but Dr. B's followers have continued to join us. He's calling them his Silver Legion. Nevertheless, we are here on Earth 3, which means we only have to get through this world and Earth 2 to get to the Prime World! Dr. B and I are eager to find the next portal and will begin searching right away!

Earth-3
1998
50 Years Ago

We have spent about two Earth-3 years looking for this portal. Fun fact about this world: an Earth-3 day is only twenty-four hours. It has been consistently like this since Earth-15, which is weird, but what's even weirder is that since I'm from Earth-216, I'm over 600 years old in Earth-3 years. Dr. B, being from Earth-2089, is over 1000 Earth-3 years old. Anyway, we have spent two of these Earth-3 years looking for this portal to Earth-2, which is pretty normal. Like I said before, the past twelve Earths have all been twenty-four-hour day Earths, and it took us about four of those Earth years to find the portal. Mainly thanks to Dr. B's Silver Legion. If it was just me and him, this would take forever. I know that might seem confusing, so to sum up, we are on schedule to find the portal to Earth-2!

Earth-3
March 16, 2000
48 Years Ago

We've been looking for this portal for four years now. An average amount of time to find one of these. I'm still optimistic, but Dr. B clearly isn't. We've searched six of the seven continents. It has to be in North America. It has to be. Right now, we are looking around St. Louis, Missouri, in the United States, but Dr. B is just losing it, acting out; I mean, he's acting like a child. The

Silver Legion has just been a joke. I never really liked the Silver Legion, but at least in the past they helped us find the portals. Now? You'd be lucky to see one of them simply looking around.

We have also found this bar to relax at during the night. Tonight, Dr. B, some members of the Silver Legion, and I went to this bar. It wasn't very crowded, though at that point it hadn't been too late into the night. I saw some people sitting at their tables, and some people playing pool in the back corner. The lights were sparse; a neon-blue sign behind the bar illuminated the text *Bob's Bar*, and that neon-blue washed over the bar.

I grabbed a seat at the bar and asked for a Moscow Mule, the bartender gave a nod in reply. Suddenly, I could clearly hear everything around me, as if I had been sleeping until I ordered that drink. I could hear the clanks of glasses and the people's conversations all around me. I watched as the bartender slid my drink down the bar, and I watched as it slowly came to a stop right in front of me. I looked at the bartender, and we exchanged nods. I looked down at the drink, the copper mug, the clear liquid with chunks of ice floating at the top, and a lime, a soft green lime on the edge of the mug.

I was brought back to reality by a faint touch on my shoulder. I turned around to see the most beautiful woman I have ever lay my eyes upon. She was short, a little over five feet tall; she had long curly brown hair and a long black dress on. She asked, "Is anyone sitting there?" She pointed to the empty seat right next to me.

"By all means." I waved my hand over the seat.

She smiled, sat down, and said, "I'm Ava."

"Edward."

"Are you here alone, Edward?" she asked.

I looked over to the corner of the bar where Dr. B had been sulking all night. I pointed to Dr. B and said, "Just him."

She turned to look at Dr. B. Her eyes widened as she asked, "Oh are you—"

I immediately knew what she was going to say. Idiot, *Just him*. Why did I say that? That's not what she meant. "Oh no, we're just friends."

She chuckled. "Ah, I see." She glanced down at the table and said, "Moscow Mule? That's a good one." She waved down at the bartender and pointed to my drink. "I'll have the same," she said, and I smiled.

We talked for jeez I don't know how long. But our conversation was cut short. Dr. B noticed us, which is fine, but I guess he got mad because he came up to me, grabbed my arm, and said, "We have to get back to work," before yanking me out of the bar. I just don't understand him sometimes.

The weird thing is I keep thinking of her, of that moment. I have been across 200 Earths parallel to this one, and yet that night was the first night in a long time where I felt calm, where I felt like me again. And I liked it.

Earth-3
March 17, 2000
48 Years Ago

This morning, Dr. B left a note saying he was going off alone to look for the portal. I'm fine with this because he has been kind of a dick the last couple of days. All day I kept thinking about last night, about her, about that feeling.

Tonight, I went to the bar, to chase that feeling. I saw Ava sitting, alone, right in front of me at the bar table. I walked up to her, faintly tapped her on the shoulder, and asked, "Is anyone sitting there?"

So that's how they met, Luke thought, almost forgetting about the dead body right in front of him. He turned the page in the journal to see a Post-it note covering the page. The Post-it note read, "If you're reading this, flip to the final page." Luke furrowed his brow as he flipped to the final pages of the journal. He took glances at them. They were letters. He saw one for Dr. B, one for Barry White, and one for him. The very last page in his father's journal was a letter to him.

Dear Luke,

My son, there's something I've been wanting to talk to you about. Something I've been needing to talk to you for a long time about but I just haven't been able to. I don't know why, truly. And it's not that I don't trust you. I trust you, and I love you, and I need you to know that.

If you're looking in this, that means you most likely have read some if not all of my journal, which means you know things, things I never really wanted you to know, not because you didn't deserve to know but because you were better off not knowing. At Least that's what I thought, but what do I know?

If you're reading this, that means you know I'm not from this world, and you know that very fact is what killed your mother a year after you were born. It's not your fault, and it's not her fault; if anything, it's mine, at least that's what Tim or, I guess in your case, Dr. B seems to think.

Dr. B hated me after I met your mom. I fell in love. He didn't, and he hated me for it.

If you're reading this, you might be confused about where I'm from. Basically, there is an infinite number of Earths. Earth one, Earth two, Earth three, etcetera, and the only way to travel between these Earths is numerically. For example, son, the only way to get to Earth one from Earth three is through Earth two. Dr. B seems to think that Earth one, also known as the Prime World, holds all the knowledge of the universe because it was made first. So he has made it his life's mission to travel to the Prime World all the way from Earth-2089. Each Earth he went to, he gained followers, people who saw the same vision as him. Soon he gained so many followers that it could be classified as an army on most Earths. He named this army the Silver Legion, and I naively joined him when he came to my Earth.

If you're reading this, then I am dead. And I saw it coming, most likely from Dr. B, someone I used to consider a brother. I still do. The truth is, Luke, when I joined the Silver Legion, I wasn't thinking straight. At first, I felt a sense of purpose, but then I didn't feel anything at all. For years, I felt numb and somehow tight at the same time, and then your mom tapped me on the shoulder, and for the first time in a long time, I started to feel things again. I started to feel happy. And that's why I've stayed here for so long because even after your mom died, I still had you.

If you're reading this, then I want you to know something, Luke, something that took me my entire life to learn. For the longest time, I ran. I ran from my home, from my people, from my feelings, from my Earth, and you might think to yourself it's easier to run, especially if you're running from something you don't like, running from that feeling, that scary deadly feeling deep down inside of you. And to face that feeling can be seen as giving up your life or freedom. You might think it's easier to run. And it is. But I didn't raise a boy who takes the easy way out. I raised a boy who stands his ground and fights for what he thinks is right even if it seems impossible. I raised a boy who confronts his destiny and doesn't run from it. I raised you, Luke.

CHAPTER 18

Perspective

Alex and Zack were across the room from Luke quietly talking next to the microscope.

"Check this out," Alex said to Zack, who was walking toward him. From Alex's point of view, Luke still looked like he was reading his father's journal.

"What is it?" Zack asked.

"Well, you know that liquid we found in the fake bullet?"

"Yeah."

"I took a sample of it and put it under here," Alex pointed to the microscope, "and I think I know what it is."

"Well, what is it?"

Alex walked over to the bookshelf next to where the fire extinguisher was supposed to be, grabbed a textbook, walked back over to Zack, and dropped it onto the table. "Look in there." Alex pointed to the microscope as he flipped through the textbook. Zack leaned his head in toward it, clearly not knowing what to do, but Alex didn't seem to notice. "You're going to find C12H9NS," Alex said as he flipped the textbook open about one hundred more pages, "also known as phenothiazine." Alex pointed to it in the textbook. "You look closer, and you'll find thioxanthenes, butyrophenones, clozapine, and rauwolfia alkaloids." Alex pointed to all of them in the book.

"Those words mean nothing to me."

"Those are the basic ingredients for a tranquilizer."

Zack's eyes widened. "Holy shit! That guard…in the courtyard."

"They're not killing these kids! They're kidnapping them!"

"What about these kids?" Zack was referring to the kids who got blown up in the classroom.

"Maybe they saw who killed Edward? Maybe they saw who was behind all of this?" Alex said.

"It's the band!" Luke said from across the room. "Or Dr. B or his army."

"Whose army?" Alex asked.

"Dr. B's army. He calls them the Silver Legion," Luke answered.

"The marching band?" Alex whispered to Zack.

"Annie told Logan she had band practice," Zack concluded.

"And I think I know where he took them," Luke said.

"What the hell was in that journal?" Alex asked.

"We need to go!" Zack said as he hastily started walking to the door. "The Silver Legion is coming," said the warning from the computer. It wasn't the marching band; it was an army.

Luke got up, slowly started walking to the door, squeezed his father's journal into his chest, and answered Alex's question while looking at the ground. "My father left me a letter."

Zack slowed his pace, closed his eyes, and sighed.

"What did it say?" Alex followed Zack to the door.

Luke looked up toward Zack as he answered, "To not run."

Zack stopped walking, looked back at Luke, and then looked at Edward and then back at Luke.

"Well, that just seems unhealthy," Alex said.

Zack scoffed before asking, "Is everyone ready?"

"No, where are we going?" Luke asked.

"To get out of this school!"

"But all the doors are locked, aren't they?" Alex asked.

"Where we're going, we don't need doors!" Zack said.

"Logan's truck!" Luke's eyes widened.

"Did you steal that from back to the future?" Alex asked Zack.

"We're leaving," Zack said blatantly as he opened the classroom door.

CHAPTER 19

The Eye of Nature

Logan was sitting on the toilet, as if it was a throne, in the stall he was hiding in when he crashed his truck into the side of the school. A part of him regretted throwing the vape away in the tunnels below. Right outside of Logan's stall, Aidan was pacing back and forth, those gunshots banging over and over again in his head. On the far wall, Nate was sitting down, his jaw trembling and his eyes pointed straight forward watching Kody fall to the ground over and over again in his head. Preston was standing over the sink, washing his hands. He walked over next to the paper towel dispenser, which was next to the bathroom door exit. Preston dried his hands and looked back at his friends. None of them seemed to notice him, so he carefully walked out of the bathroom and toward the courtyard.

*****

Zack, Alex, and Luke carefully ran through the halls that lead to the commons. Even as they carefully ran through the commons, there was no sign of any guards. *Guards still must be collecting bodies,* Alex thought, assuming Luke and Zack were thinking the same thing. They walked past the main office, where Sally the secretary once was, and down the hall that led to Logan's truck halfway through the wall. Alex and Luke went ahead of Zack and into the classroom with Logan's truck in it. Zack stayed outside of the classroom and stopped in front of the men's restroom right next to it. He furrowed his brow and leaned in closer to the door.

"Where did he go!" One voice yelled.

"I don't know. He was here just a second ago!" Another voice yelled back.

"Relax, you guys, he probably just went out to take a hit or a shit or something." A third voice added, although this voice sounded familiar.

Was it, "Logan?" Zack asked, slowly opening the door. The bathroom went silent.

Zack slowly walked forward, peaking around the corner to see Logan, whose arms were open wide, stomped toward him, and shouted, "Zackie poo!" Logan wrapped his arms around Zack and tried to lift him into the air but failed miserably.

"Weren't there five of you?" Zack asked.

"Kody didn't make it," Nate said.

They all got quiet for a second.

"Oh," Zack said, "I'm sorry." Zack took a moment before asking, "What happened to your fifth?"

"We don't know where Preston is," Aidan said.

"Shit." Zack sighed, under his breath. He looked back up at the three helpless kids. "Well, come on, let's get you out of here."

Meanwhile, Alex and Luke went into the classroom with Logan's truck in it.

Alex said, "Come on, let's go!" not realizing Zack wasn't behind them. Alex hopped into the driver's seat, punched his fist through a panel below the steering wheel, and started messing with the wires coming out of it.

Luke, on the other hand, tried to hop into the passenger's seat but was blocked by a bunch of bags filled with white powder that he had to push onto the ground. He took a seat, set his father's journal on the floor, and looked into the classroom, absolutely destroyed with dust filling the air. The light from the outside could be seen shining through the dusty destroyed classroom, and yet Luke could still see it, something he hadn't seen in a long time, the eye of nature itself sitting calmly in a classroom.

Back in the bathroom, Zack led Logan, Nate, and Aidan out of the bathroom. As soon as Nate, who was at the front of the line, exited the bathroom, a rain of gunfire blasted toward him. One of the bullets shot through his calf, making him fall to the ground. Aidan, who was right behind Nate, lifted his arms under Nate's shoulders and dragged him to the classroom. Logan followed Aidan, but Zack stayed in the doorway, gunfire to his left and hopeless souls to his right.

Luke saw Aidan drag Nate into the classroom. Luke got out of the passenger's seat and ran over to them.

"Help me pick him up!" Aidan told Luke, nodding his head toward Nate. Without question, Luke helped Aidan, and together they carried Nate onto the bed of the truck. Logan ran past Alex and hopped into the bed of the truck with Nate, waving his arms in the air the whole time.

The rumble of the engine could be heard starting up as Alex popped his head out and yelled, "It's time to go!" As he said it, he could see Zack running through the doorway, with gunfire raining behind him. Luke hopped back into the passenger's seat and put his seatbelt on.

Zack ran past Alex and shouted as he hopped into the bed of the truck, "Drive!"

As fast as a blink, Alex had that truck in reverse, and his foot slammed on the gas. At first the truck didn't go anywhere, and the tires just screeched, kicking up smoke into the already dusty room, but half a second later, that truck was flying out of that building. The soldiers made it to the doorway and started blasting bullets toward the truck, shattering the windshield. Everyone reacted by jolting their heads down. Alex turned the truck, saw the police on top of the hill in front of the school, put the car in drive, and slammed on the gas again, launching them toward the police. One second later, Alex had driven to the top of the hill and was slamming on the brakes, trying not to crash into one of the police cars.

"Ah, yo, what are we doing? These psychos killed Kody!" Logan spat out.

"Relax," Zack said stoically.

They were maybe one hundred feet away from the school building at this point. All the police officers looked scared and confused.

Zack was the only one who looked like he had a fire in his soul as he hopped out of the bed of the truck, walked over to the closest police office to him, and swung a punch right in the police officer's face, knocking him to the ground.

CHAPTER 20

Who We Are

"Coward!" Zack yelled to the officer he put to the ground. He looked up at the rest of them, pointed, and said, "All of you!"

A police officer came from Zack's right, shoved him back toward the truck, and said, "Don't you dare touch one of my boys like that!"

Zack walked back up to him, got up in his face, and said softly, "Or what?"

In the blink of an eye, the police officer pulled out his gun and put it underneath Zack's chin, "Ill blow your damn brains out!"

Neither Zack nor the police officer moved, not even a twitch. Alex and Luke stared at the standoff. Aidan, who was in the bed of the truck, tried to help Nate with his bullet wound. Logan was passed out right next to them.

Half a second later, Zack snatched the gun out of the police officer's hand as fast as a cheetah snatches its prey and pointed it at the police officer. "I'd love to see you try." Zack gave the police officer a smirk as the rest of the police officers pulled their guns out and aimed them at Zack. Zack's smirk faded instantly, and he gave an annoyed sigh.

"Wait, boys," the police officer said and in front of Zack raised his hand, "remember the plan."

"The plan? What plan?" Zack asked hastily.

The police officer smiled and started to walk backward as the police officers behind him put their guns down. Luke squinted his eyes, focusing on Zack as he kept his gun out. Zack looked around, noticing all the police officers doing the same thing, lowering their guns almost all at the same time. Zack scoffed, lowered his gun, and said, "Cowards."

Luke shook his head and opened the passenger door to get out of the truck.

"Luke, what are you doing?" Alex asked, but Luke ignored him, got out of the truck, and slammed the passenger's seat door shut. Aidan popped his head out to see Alex get out of the truck as well. Aidan saw Alex do it, so he did the same.

"So are you!" Luke said, looking directly at Zack.

Zack shook his head, trying to focus on the police officers and Luke. "Excuse me?"

"You're a DAMN coward!" Luke said.

Alex's jaw dropped. "Oh, shit."

"I'm a coward?" Zack scoffed, pointing to himself and turning toward Luke.

Luke pointed to the school. "We now know what's happening. We know who did it. We know why he did it."

"We don't know anything!"

"We know all of those kids," Luke pointed to the school, "who we thought died are alive somewhere in that school, and yet you still chose to run away!"

"So WE COULD SURVIVE!" Zack screamed, and a long silence followed. Calmly and softly, Zack said, "There is no shame in running, not today."

They all stood silently for a moment.

"And we don't know the why," Alex stated.

"What?" Luke asked.

Alex looked around, amazed no one saw what he saw. "Well, unless it was in that journal and you just didn't tell us, but you just told us it was Dr. B and his army. You never told us why."

"Yeah, that's because I didn't read 'Why!'" Luke snapped back.

"In the tunnels," Aidan said, stepping forward, "beneath the school, we saw this room with what looked to be a bunch of dead students piled up on each other and…and at the end of this room, there was this portal."

"Portal?" Luke asked.

"Yeah, it was blue and—"

"Had the number three at the top," Luke and Aidan said at the same time.

"How did you—" Aidan began to ask.

"My dad wrote about it. Alex, you said the bullets had tranquilizer in them?" Luke asked.

"Yeah and…oh my gosh!"

Luke shook his head as he said, "They're not killing these kids. They're kidnapping them and throwing them through that portal."

"We gotta get down there!" Aidan said.

"Do you remember the way?" Luke asked.

"Of course. I can—"

"Wait!" Zack interrupted. "You're not going down there!"

Luke sighed. "If there is chance that Preston is down there, if Mike is down there, if Annie"—Zack looked down—"is down there. If any kid is alive and down there, tell me, would it not be worth it to go down there and save them?"

Zack lowered his head.

"Sometimes, courage is knowing there could be trouble and taking the chance anyway."

Zack looked up at Luke. "That's the definition of stupidity." Zack started to blink heavily, and a tear started to fall down his face. "I wanted to be just like him. To save people." He shook his head. "But I couldn't even save a couple of kids. If he were here, he would have saved the school." Another tear fell down Zack's face. "Because he was a hero."

"Zack," Luke said, "you didn't have to save the school. You just had to save the people. The Silver Legion attacked, and everyone lost all hope. All they needed was someone to stand up and fight for them. That someone was supposed to be you, and now, we know it's not too late."

Zack looked at the gun in his hand and then at Luke and smiled. He looked over at Alex. "You take Logan and what's his name—"

"Nate!" Aidan interrupted.

"Whatever. Take them to the nearest hospital. You two." Zack pointed to Luke and Aidan, sighed, and said, "Let's go get this son of a bitch."

"Follow me," Aidan said, and they walked back down toward the school with ease.

Alex hopped back in the truck, put it in reverse, turned around, and drove off without the police interfering at all. Alex looked in the rear-view mirror at the police officers as he drove farther away. Alex knew something was up, and if the police were involved, who else in this city was?

The police officer whose gun Zack stole walked over to the edge of the hill in front of the school, pulled out a walkie-talkie, and said, "They're coming right down!" as Aidan, Luke, and Zack walked down the stairs that led to the portal underneath the school.

CHAPTER 21

Mr. Dorris

Aidan, Luke, and Zack burst through the double doors and walked down the metal stairs with no interruptions. Zack was in the middle, holding up his gun, while Aidan led the way, and Luke followed closely behind. They walked down the metal stairs slowly silently and, each step, cursed.

They arrived at the bottom of the stairs, a few feet away from the corner that led to the portal room. Aidan whispered, "It's around that corner!" Zack got in front of him. Luke and Aidan huddled behind Zack as he slowly creeped forward and turned the corner, his gun pointing straight ahead.

"Well, well, well, Mr. Dorris, you were right." Dr. B stood in the middle of the room, his hands resting on Preston's shoulders. Zack's gun pointed right at Dr. B, who seemed to have no reaction to it. There were piles of kids lying unconscious on each side of the room and a big blue portal with the number three at the top looming behind Dr. B. A deep hum radiated throughout the room. "Although it's not all of them, oh," Dr. B waved it off, "I'll just have my boys out front take care of them for me." Dr. B looked up at the balcony to his right. Six soldiers all had their guns pointed at Aidan, Luke, and Zack. "Do one of you mind telling them for me please?" He waved his pointer finger at the soldiers on the balcony. Soldiers also poured in behind Aidan, Luke, and Zack and surrounded them everywhere except for in front of them, where Preston, Dr. B, and the big blue portal stood.

So, the police were also Dr. B's, Zack thought, but he didn't have time to confront Dr. B about that. "Let the kid go!" Zack had the gun pointed right at Dr. B's head.

"Oh!" Dr. B let go of Preston, waving his fingers in the air, but Preston didn't move. "My apologies, I didn't realize we were not allowed to do that anymore. Touching kids and all, and you know what, I just heard it. I can see the confusion. It won't happen again."

"Preston, come on. What are you doing?" Luke asked.

"Oh, you know, this also must be confusing," Dr. B said, waving his pointer finger at Luke and Preston.

"Annie," Zack said.

"I guess it wasn't that confusing," Preston told Dr. B.

"I guess not!" Dr. B gave a cocky smile.

"Preston, what the hell!" Aidan shouted.

"You guys don't get it. You don't see his vision. The Prime World is two portal hops away. You can taste the perfection from here!" Preston said.

"Then why don't you just go? You and your little legion?" Zack asked, shaking the gun around to point at all the soldiers surrounding them.

"We ran into a problem," Dr. B said. "The second world is filled with…monsters, one might say. Hundreds of thousands of monsters all surrounding the portal to the Prime World. I needed an army to kill these monsters and make a path to the portal so I can finally get to the Prime World."

"It seems to me you have an army," Luke said.

Dr. B gave a quick smile. "Not the Silver Legion, not my army, but a disposable army, and kids in a small town were the perfect corporate, and I've been growing it for…oh, years. Car crashes—"

Zack remembered Ian Kelsay and the car crash a couple months ago that Sally, the secretary, had mentioned.

"Missing students—" Dr. B added.

Zack's mind shot to Annie who had just been missing for a couple of days.

"But it was too slow." Dr. B added.

"So you staged a school shooting?" Zack asked.

"B-b-bingo," Preston said. "Does he get a prize?"

"It's happening everywhere else, right? Why not here?" Dr. B asked.

"And you agree with this psychopath?" Luke asked, looking at Preston.

"The first world ever created…it has to be perfect, technologically advanced beyond our wildest dreams. If it's the first world, then it's been around the longest, which means it's miles ahead in everything!"

"You're insane!" Luke said.

"Your father thought the same thing. Guess ignorance runs through the family!"

"Hey, you better watch it!" Zack yelled, putting his finger on the trigger and pointing it toward Dr. B.

All the soldiers stiffened up. "Or what?" Dr. B asked. "You know, while we're on the subject of your father," Dr. B pointed to Luke with a flexed arm, "for years, I used to hate that he ran off with that WHORE, and it wasn't until I killed him that I realized that I didn't need him at all." Luke's face lost all emotion. Aidan's and Zack's jaws dropped as Dr. B continued. "All that loneliness was exactly what I needed to kick my ass into gear and get to fucking work."

Without hesitation, Zack pulled the trigger with the barrel aimed right at Dr. B's head. The bang echoed through the room. Smoke poured out of the gun, blocking Zack's sight, but out of the smoke, Dr. B still stood there with not a hole in him. It was a blank.

"You think I'd be dumb enough to bring you down here with a loaded gun?" Dr. B asked.

"What?" Zack exhaled and pulled the trigger three more times. *Bang, bang, bang!* All blanks.

"Haven't you figured it out yet?" Dr. B asked as he walked toward Zack, who was still trying to shoot Dr. B, but the only thing that came out of that barrel were more blanks. "The police work for me!" Dr. B grabbed the barrel of the gun and yanked it out of Zack's hands. Zack's jaw trembled as he stood there frozen. Dr. B emptied the magazine and reloaded the gun, this time with real bullets. "Everyone does!" Dr. B raised the gun and shot Zack right between the eyes. Aidan and Luke jumped back in fright, right into one of the soldiers' barrels, which caused them to leap forward almost stepping on Zack, whose body was now lying on the ground in a pool of blood.

Dr. B nodded his head, waved his finger, pointing at Aidan and Luke, and said, "Send them through." Within half a second, they both got shot, which was immediately followed by them passing out and falling to the floor.

*****

The first thing Luke felt when he woke up was the cold stickiness of mud engulfing him. The place he was at was dark, and he could barely see anything, except for what was right in front of him. He looked up, realizing he was lying on the muddy ground, and saw a girl standing in front of him.

Luke squinted his eyes as he looked up.

"Annie?" Luke asked.

"Hey, Luke," said Annie.

ABOUT THE AUTHOR

Joshua Mancini is the famous author of one whole book, but this is his second! His previous works include, and is limited to, *Mind of McDavid*, released when the author was only in high school. Now, Joshua Mancini is a sophomore in college pursuing a degree in philosophy.